THE SURVIVALIST

#36

OPERATION PHOENIX

Books in The Survivalist Series by Jerry Ahern

#1: Total War
#2: The Nightmare Begins
#3: The Quest
#4: The Doomsayer
#5: The Web
#6: The Savage Horde
#7: The Prophet
#8: The End is Coming
#9: Earth Fire
#10: The Awakening
#11: The Reprisal
#12: The Rebellion
#13: Pursuit
#14: The Terror
#15: Overlord

Mid-Wake
#16: The Arsenal
#17: The Ordeal
#18: The Struggle
#19: Final Rain
#20: Firestorm
#21: To End All War
The Legend
#22: Brutal Conquest
#23: Call To Battle
#24: Blood Assassins
#25: War Mountain
#26: Countdown
#27: Death Watch

Books in The Survivalist series by
Jerry Ahern, Sharon Ahern and Bob Anderson
#30: The Inheritors of Earth
#31: Earth Shine
#32: The Quisling Covenant
#33: Deep Star
#34 Lodestar
#35 Blood Moon

The Rourke Chronicles by
Jerry Ahern, Sharon Ahern and Bob Anderson
#1 Everyman
#2 Demons and Monsters

Books by Sean Ellis
Camp Zero
(*Camp Zero* series is based on characters created by Jerry Ahern, Sharon Ahern and Bob Anderson in *The Survivalist* series.)

Coming Soon
Icefall, Book II in the *Camp Zero* series

THE SURVIVALIST

#36

OPERATION PHOENIX

Jerry Ahern
Sharon Ahern
Bob Anderson

SPEAKING VOLUMES, LLC
NAPLES, FLORIDA
2019

THE SURVIVALIST
#36 OPERATION PHOENIX

Editing assistance provided by Pamela Anderson and Steven Servello.

Content in Chapter Seventy-One is based on information described in the book *On Killing*, by Dave Grossman.

ISBN 978-1-64540-034-9

On October 12, 2018, the knife world lost one of its true greats when Russell Knives announced, "A.G. Russell exchanged his earthly life for eternal peace with his Lord Jesus Christ. During what was supposed to be a routine angiogram to check for blockage in a coronary artery, A. G. Russell's heart gave out and he left this world.

"Just days before, A.G. had been in the office working with Phil Gibbs on knife designs and talking to customers in our store; he especially enjoyed the kiddos."

To his friends and family, A.G. was a force that will always be near to their hearts. To the rest of us, not to mention the readers of the Rourke adventures, he was a legend that touched many souls, most of whom he never actually met.

What better legacy is there?

The Phoenix

In Greek mythology the Phoenix was a long-lived bird, like an eagle only larger, that cyclically regenerated or is otherwise reborn. The Phoenix begins a new life after rising from the ashes of its predecessor. According to some sources, the Phoenix dies in a show of flames and combustion, although there are other sources that claim that the legendary bird dies and simply decomposes before being born again.

There are different traditions concerning the lifespan of the Phoenix but, by most accounts, the Phoenix lived for 500 years before rebirth.

The name is derived from Middle English before 1150 A.D., which means the concept was wide-spread. In fact, scholars have observed similarities to the Phoenix in a variety of cultures such as the Hindu Garuda and Gandaberunda, the Russian Firebird, and the Persian Simorgh; just to name a few (source: Wikipedia).

Prologue

I edged left, my eyes watching Karamatsov's eyes, the fog starting to lift and swirl as the wind picked up, sunlight breaking through. I squint, despite the glasses, against the glare of the sun on the gray fog.

It was misleading, I thought, *to say you should watch the eyes. Karamatsov had probably assumed as much. At twenty-five yards or so, the eyes themselves would be hard or impossible to see, clearly. Instead, you watched the set of the eyes,* he thought, *the almost imperceptible tightening of the muscles around them, the little squint that—*

I see his eyes set.

Karamatsov's right hand flashed up toward the Model 59 in the shoulder rig, the thumb snap breaking with an almost audible click, the gun's muzzle straightening out as Karamatsov took a half-step right and crouched, his left hand moving to help grasp the gun; the hat caught up by a gust of wind and sailing from his head.

My right hand moves first, then my left, the right hand bringing the first Detonics on line; the safety swept off under my thumb as the gun cleared the leather, the gun in the left hand moving on line as I trigger the first shot.

I see the flash against the fog of Karamatsov's pistol, the stainless Detonics bucking through recoil in my right hand, then the left gun firing, then the right and the left simultaneously.

Karamatsov flew up off the ground almost a foot, I judge, the gun in Karamatsov's hands firing up into the air—a second round. The Russian's body twitches in midair, then lurches twice more as it falls, the Russian's gun firing again into the street. A window smashes on the other side. His body rolls over face down, the right arm and left leg twitching, shivering, and then stopping.

There was no more movement.

I thumb up the safety on the pistol in my right hand and jab it into my belt, shifting the gun in my left hand to my right, thumb up the safety and hold the gun limp at my side against my thigh and walk forward, slowly, then stop, rolling over the Russian's body with my combat-booted foot, my right thumb poised over the safety of the pistol.

There are four dark-red patches on Karamatsov's trunk.

I bend over and, with the thumb of my left hand, close the eyelids.

"Done," I whisper.

Chapter One

The satellite phone chirped in General Frank Sullivan's briefcase. He pulled to the side of the road and stopped. Setting the briefcase on the seat, he thumbed the latches and pulled out the phone. There was a text message on the screen; a single word—"Marco."

Sullivan hit the erase key and smiled. Michael Rourke and the Rourke family were safe… at least for the moment.

*****

"We have to divide our forces," John Rourke said simply. "We need to have forces at more than one location to facilitate travel, protect our secrecy and to ensure if we lose some forces we don't lose all of them with one attack. Besides, here at Retreat 2, we are limited on space."

"Are you thinking about Alaska?" Michael asked.

John nodded. "It is logical. First of all, I still have no idea how extensive The Creator's base is. We do know, however, that every one of The Eggs General Thorne now has manned can hanger there and have a lot of room left over.

"There is even enough for our three VTOL's cargo birds and several of the AATVs—armored all-terrain vehicles—and a couple of ATPAAVs—all-terrain powered armored attack vehicles—to be hidden there and remain undetected with minimal effort.

"I'm thinking we have Akiro Kuriname, the pilots for The Eggs and the Dog Soldiers based there in Alaska. We keep Wes Sanderson's Marines and the POTUS Posse here with their AATVs and the majority of the ATPAAVs; that gives us mobility and logistical support at both locations."

"We have room for maybe one of the VTOLs, and maybe a small plane or two in the second cavern we discovered along with a few of the AATVs and ATPAAVs," Paul said. "Plus we have room in the main cavern for several of the ground vehicles if need be."

Rourke nodded. "This sounds reasonable to me, I'll start drawing up a listing of supplies and vehicles for transfer to… what are we going to call The Creator's location? We can't just keep calling it The Creator's Location."

"Pyramid Base sounds good," Michael said. "Speaks to us but no one else if a message is intercepted."

Chapter Two

A day later John Rourke walked to the sliding door in the tunnel and raised his hand to knock, the door slid open and The Creator walked out. He handed Rourke the headband. Rourke adjusted it and began to speak.

"How are you?"

I... am... well... how... are... you?

"Well, also."

How... may... I... be... of... assistance?

"I need to ask a favor of you. Is it permitted that we use some of your space to house some equipment and personnel? I believe it will be necessary for my people to have resources at more than one location."

You... are... expecting... there... will... be... problems... with... the... Others?

"Not all of the Others but some. There will be problems with some of my people as well, including some we call Russians. Some of the Others are our friends and I might need to provide space for them as well."

It was the only time Rourke had ever seen a physical reaction breakthrough The Creator's normal persona.

Others... here? You... wish... to... bring... Others... here?

Rourke nodded. "Yes, but not many and only ones that you have approved."

How... do... I... approve... of... Others?

"I ask that first of all, you speak with one of the Others that I know well and trust. If that meeting goes well, maybe you and he could discuss Others that would be agreeable to the both of you to have stationed here."

You... bring... that... Other... here?

"Yes."

The Creator stood impassive, the only movement was the head which periodically moved from side to side; on a human, it could have been interpreted as quizzical or thoughtful. If... you... believe... this... is... necessary... I... will... do... it... John... Rourke.

Rourke was stunned; he did not ever remember The Creator calling him by name before.

How... do... you... call... this... Other?

"He is known as The Keeper."

The Creator was silent for a moment. The... Keeper... will... be... safe... here... tell... him... that... for... me. The creature held out his hand for the headband and, receiving it, turned and returned through the sliding door.

Chapter Three

"Mr. President, we have finished our analysis of the crime scene at the Presidential residence at Hana on the eastern tip of Maui. As you know, the devastation was complete and the destruction incredible. The only good news was the end came quick... I doubt any of them were awakened or even knew they..."

"... even knew they were dead, Doctor?" President Phillip Greene dabbed at the corner of his mouth with a clean handkerchief as he smiled at the Medical Examiner's discomfort.

"Yes ...even knew they were dead, Mr. President." The Medical Examiner checked her notes. "As I said, the devastation was complete and the destruction incredible. There were no intact remains recovered."

"No intact remains... none at all?" Greene leaned forward, with new concern in his voice.

"No Sir, identification was made by DNA samples collected at the scene. With the exception of samples that remained, the bodies..."

"Doctor, what about the bodies?"

The Medical Examiner took a deep breath. "For all intents and purposes, Mr. President... the bodies were destroyed not only beyond recognition but for the most part... almost beyond even collecting."

"Then how do we know they are all..."

"Rest assured Mr. President, unfortunately, all of the Rourkes and the Rubensteins perished in the explosion and resulting fire. We have collected and analyzed DNA samples that matched President Rourke, the First Lady and their two children.

"We also have samples that match John Thomas Rourke, his wife Emma and their two children along with his former wife Sarah, and his father-in-law, Tim Shaw. Lastly, we have samples that match Paul and Annie Rubenstein and their two children.

"Luckily, room assignments within the Presidential retreat aided in identification. We have another sample that we believe is a family friend named William Estes, located in the house. Strangely there are three as yet unidentified remains that we suspect were unidentified guests staying with the President and the family.

"We have confirmed that the cause for the explosion and fire was natural gas piping that had damage... we suspect from recent seismic activity and that leaked gas into a cavity beneath the quarters. Eventually a spark ignited and... well, as I said, the devastation was complete and the destruction incredible."

"So, your report concludes this was an accident with no survivors?"

"Correct, Mr. President."

"Thank you, Doctor, I appreciate your diligence..."

"Mr. President, do you have more questions?"

Phillip Greene pondered how to phrase his next statement without arousing suspicion. "There is no way your DNA results could be wrong, Doctor? After all, you said your samples were small."

"Sorry Sir, I may have misled you, or you misinterpreted what I was trying to convey. In an explosion there is a rapid increase in the volume of gases. This results in a release of energy in an extreme manner accompanied by high temperatures and the release of gases. Sir, do you remember the Mexico City gas tragedy from twenty years ago?"

Greene nodded. "Of course..."

The M.E. nodded. "In that disaster, as in this one, cadavers recovered from the scene had massive damage, in most cases, the torso was all that remained and they weren't in the best condition. Our recovery efforts were very similar in this case."

Greene leaned forward. "Forgive me, Doctor, if I seem insensitive... I have to speak to the world and convince them there is no hope... no hope whatsoever, that the Rourkes... any of the Rourkes survived this tragedy. So you are saying you found actual bodies, not just smears of DNA material?"

"Correct, Mr. President. I can state unequivocally, the entire family and all of its members are now deceased."

Chapter Four

The new Retreat, known as Retreat 2, located at the former Fantastic Caverns just north of what had been Springfield, Missouri, had filled up fast after the "death" of the Rourkes and Rubensteins.

The vehicles and supplies that would maintain and support Operation Phoenix had been consolidated and moved to their assigned locations. Housing, Operations, Communications, Maintenance and Medical were all up and running, although not at one hundred percent of operational capacity.

When the decision was made that it was time for Operation Phoenix to go operational, preparations had not been totally complete. For three days, Paul Rubenstein had moved between the different areas checking everything from food stores to flashlight batteries to toilet paper.

Now, he and Michael Rourke, former President of the United States, sat with John Thomas Rourke, and several others in the main conference room.

"Here is everything that is currently in place within the Cavern," Paul said passing out spreadsheets. "The good news is we have almost ninety-eight percent of our stores in place. The bad news is, what we have is what we have and it will have to be rationed out. The worse news is, we don't know how long we are going to have to be here and that means we don't know how long to make these supplies last."

"Paul, what about the resupply measures we had talked about?" John Rourke queried.

"I think they can still remain in play… I just don't know how long it will be before they can be activated."

Paul stood. "Monitoring the news feeds concerning our deaths… well, the bad news is the outside world is in turmoil. The good news is it appears that 'our deaths' were convincing enough. We are dead to the world."

Michael said, "President Franklin had created what he called, the Lockout Team. It consisted of high ranking military and civilian leaders from a wide circle of influence dedicated to the Constitution and the continuation of the United States. Lockout is still operational but with the restructuring of the government that President Phillip Greene initiated... well, it will be a while before we can determine how operational it will actually be."

*****

The meeting had lasted a little over four hours. The consensus was while things were in "pretty good shape" overall, finite supplies remained a concern for the long term. John Rourke had reminded Rubenstein how they had resupplied themselves while on their journey after The Night of the War.

"Whenever any of our people are outside and away from Retreat 2, they must be vigilant for supplies of all kinds," he concluded. "If they don't have the availability to bring those 'found' resources back to Retreat 2, they should conceal them so we can retrieve them later."

Finally, the others departed and just Michael, Paul and John were left around the table. "Okay, I think we should talk about the children now," Michael said.

"I think the ladies ought to be here for this discussion," Paul stated.

John nodded. "Emma is not in the shape to participate, as you know. I think under the circumstances, Sarah should take her place in the discussions. I also think that the kids themselves should be involved in the final decisions.

Michael and Paul agreed. Paul said, "I think there should be another person involved, Otto Croenberg. I've spoken with Natalie and John Michael... there is a pretty significant bond that has developed between the kids and Otto... or should I say 'Uncle' Otto.

John smirked. "'Uncle' Otto?"

"Yes, 'Uncle' Otto," Michael said, smiling. I agree, he needs to be there for the final decision. Let's get our wives and Mom over here. Dad, how is Emma?"

John Rourke's smile disappeared. "Physically she's fine, Michael. Mentally and emotionally... she's broken. My friend, Dr. David Blackman, Chief of Psychological Research at Mid-Wake, has examined her and diagnosed her as having a dissociative fugue.

"It's a fairly rare psychiatric disorder affecting a person's identity, including that person's memories, personality, and other identifying characteristics of individuality. Usually it is short-lived, ranging from hours to days, but in her case it might last months or... even years. We just don't know yet.

"Look, I think we are all pretty much on board with sending the kids back to the school. And I think we are all concerned about how to do it and give them the most experience in a safe manner. I have a suggestion. Let's break up for right now, I want to talk with a couple of people. How about I set up another meeting in a while?"

Chapter Five

It had been over a month since General Rodney Thorne had walked slowly to the front of the classroom and stood.

"Gentlemen, today's lesson is on ACM or aerial combat maneuvering. All of you have been through this before and trust me… you'll go through it again. Senior pilots must teach and convey the skills necessary for their young compatriots to learn so they, one day, will become senior pilots instead of burned out holes in the ground."

These were the survivors of the intense pilot training course designed to teach airplane pilots how to fly aircraft designed by alien intelligence. Thorne knew it could be done because he had figured it out all by himself. Now, he must try to teach these skills to others. *And where should I start*, he had asked himself and had decided… *how about at the start?*

"The rules for aircraft warfare began during World War I. Aircraft were used to spot enemy troop concentrations, movements, and gun positions. The earliest aerial combat consisted of aviators shooting at one another with hand-held weapons. In fact, the first recorded aircraft to be shot down by another aircraft, occurred on October 5, 1914. The pilot was shot by an observer in the enemy plane firing a bolt action rifle.

"This single incident was the predicator for the development of fighter planes. Forward-firing machine guns were the most effective armament on a majority of World War I era fighter planes. However, since it was nearly impossible to fire them through the spinning propeller of one's own aircraft, more pilots shot down their own plane than their enemies.

"After much experimentation, a reliable system finally was implemented. A German WWI Ace was the first to publish the basic rules for ACM—aerial combat maneuvering—or dog fighting as it came to be known. He advised pilots to attack from the direction of the sun—toward which the defending pilot could not see—or to fly at a higher altitude than the opponent. Most of these rules are still as valuable today as they were almost eight centuries ago.

"Today's air combat is much more complicated than that of older times, primarily due to technology. This includes air-to-air missiles, radar, and automatic cannons capable of high rates of fire which are used on virtually all modern fighter aircraft.

"Now, flying in The Eggs eliminates most of the limiting factors a fighter pilot encounters. Remember, most kills can be attributed to the attacker spotting and shooting the defender without ever being seen. Structural limitations of the attacking fighters, us, no longer need be taken into account. Things such as thrust-to-weight ratio, wing loading, and the 'corner speed'— the maximum or minimum speed at which the aircraft can attain the best turning performance—don't count in The Egg.

"But we still must be aware of where our wingman is located and we must have good communication. The master rule is still the same, it has not changed. It was created during World War I and is still just as relevant and applicable today: Do not let your opponent get onto your six, while YOU are attempting to get on his. Now, shall we begin…?"

Chapter Six

"Hello, Mr. President..." Peter Vale said, smoothly.

"Hello and how are you?" Phillip Greene asked. What he wondered was, *How the hell did you get this number?*

"Just checking to make sure all is going according to plan," Vale said in a friendly voice.

"Ah... yes, as a matter of fact I received the final report from the Medical Examiner an hour ago and was about to call you and tell you about it." Greene dabbed at the corner of his mouth with a clean napkin, *Damn Michael Rourke to hell.*

"So... tell me?"

"It is unequivocal and the M.E. is certain that the Rourkes and the Rubensteins and one other party all died during the explosion and fire." Greene wiped the sweat from his brow.

"No questions... no possibilities of a mistake?"

Greene smiled, saying, "DNA evidence confirmed... The Rourkes and Rubensteins are gone... may they roast in hell."

"May they roast in hell," Vale echoed. "Okay, Mr. President... let's move on to the next phase since we know the Rourkes are no longer in the way."

Chapter Seven

NEWS ALERT, "Eyewitness News brings you a developing story... Ladies and Gentlemen, satellite feeds are showing a series of massive explosions in space. At first reports, these explosions appear to be in close proximity to the location of the KI Armada centered above the South Pole at a distance of 600 miles above the earth's surface." The Keeper had pushed his way into the room.

Chief of Staff Frank Sullivan and everyone else stared at the screen. "It is true then," Sullivan said.

The Keeper nodded. "I am afraid so, General. Something terrible has happened. Something terrible..."

Sullivan had caught The Keeper and eased him into a chair. "Keeper, tell me what you know."

"General, there is no time left..." The Keeper stopped and closed his eyes for a long moment. The only sound in the room was his labored, rhythmic breathing. Finally, he smiled weakly. "Forgive me, General. I am afraid circumstances have unnerved me more than I imagined."

"Keeper, tell me what you know," Sullivan said again.

The Keeper took another deep breath. "There has been an attack on my people. I do not have the full details yet, but there has been significant damage and great loss of life."

Sullivan frowned. "There have been no reports of launches directed at the KI..."

The Keeper shook his head. "No, General... no rockets or missiles... Apparently, for some while, the Russians brought in by Colonel Mikhail Sergeyevich and The Captain had been secreting devices inside our ships... explosive devices."

"I thought the KI and the Russians were supposed to be allies."

The Keeper seemed very old and very tired. "Apparently, The Captain overestimated his ability to sway the Russians and underestimated their treachery. Our security forces are intensely searching to ensure there are no more explosives. I pray there are not, the devastation is… several ships were totally destroyed, most of the others are damaged… some significantly. The death toll—appalling."

Chapter Eight

The encrypted satellite phone at the Retreat's Communication Center chirped. The Technician answered, "Yes?" Listening, he sat up straighter. "I understand, I will have him here shortly. Ten minutes will be acceptable, Sir."

He hung up and scribbled a note and handed it to his assistant. "Take this to Mr. Rourke please and hurry."

"Which one?"

"Dr. Rourke and hurry."

*****

"What is the damage?" John Thomas Rourke asked The Keeper.

"Two ships were totally destroyed by the initial blasts, several others damaged and the death toll keeps climbing. Right now it is at 3,000 but..." Wearily The Keeper continued, "... but there will be many more."

"What can we do to help?"

"Very little, I am afraid," The Keeper said. "We are consolidating personnel on those ships with the least amount of damage. Were the circumstance on the surface of the planet different... we would land and try to deal with the situation more intelligently. But with the attacks by the Russian forces and the KI forces loyal to them... we can't."

"I ask again, what can we do to help?"

The Keeper looked at Sullivan, who nodded. "Your General Sullivan has explained the situation to me and the dangers involved. It is regretful that your son is no longer in power as the President. It is unfortunate that we both seem to find ourselves and our peoples in such difficult circumstances. I ask that you do your best to protect those of my people I sent to you and those aircraft."

Rourke shook his head, not knowing what else to say. "I promise."

"Then, John Rourke... this must be the last communication of this type we shall have for a while. This is too easily listened in on. I cannot take such chances with the safety of my people. We shall talk again and soon."

"I understand... Be safe," Rourke said and the connection was broken.

Chapter Nine

John Rourke had finished his research on how to send the kids safely back to Camp Zero and had asked for that next meeting to take place. "Okay, now… the big question and the hardest decisions. How do we protect the kids and how and who are we going to task to do that?" Paul asked.

John raised his hand. "I have a volunteer, in fact maybe two of them."

"I'm all ears," Michael said.

"Otto Croenberg for one, your mother is the other," John said. "I have spoken to Otto and he has agreed. For the safety of the kids and her own sanity, I suggest your mother goes with them."

Michael spoke up, "We have created impenetrable identities for all of them. The kids have already bonded with Otto, and I think my mother has also. Outside of one of us, I can't think of anyone I'd trust more with all of them."

Michael and Paul agreed. Paul said, "I want to get the kids and Otto and Sarah settled as quickly as possible with secure identities. Once we begin our activities, they could be in danger here with us."

Michael," John said, "would you mind talking to your mom about this idea? I think it would be better received from you than me."

"She'll know it was you anyway but… yeah, I can do it." Michael frowned. "When do we want to implement them leaving? If we are agreed, I suggest we get Natalia and Annie in on this right now for their input or I think we'd be making a mistake. Paul, can you call Annie and ask her to get Natalia and come on over?"

"Sure."

"Dad, I think it would be best if Paul and I handle this with Annie and Natalia. If they agree, when do you think we should plan for the kids to go back?"

John stood to leave and said, "How about after the weekend? I'd like some time with them because we don't know when we'll get the next chance. Call me when the four of you have made a decision, you know my feelings."

Chapter Ten

The aerial battle had been devastating. For the first time in recorded history, Alien technology was being used in defense of mankind.

As the KI ships descended from orbit they were joined by Russian fighter planes. Russian Air Force Lieutenant Colonel Viktor Arkady, had surveyed his screen, given orders to his squadron and sent the Mikoyan MiG-122 into a vertical climb pulling more G's than he had ever experienced. Behind and on either side, his squadron mates slashed through clouds to both meet their allies and gain the high position before turning and joining the battle.

Mid-Wake Air Defense Command scrambled six fighters, led by Colonel Nelson Riddle. Riddle's Red, Blue and Green Flight Leaders, and their three wingmen splashed three of the Russian MiGs and damaged two of the KI craft to the point they were forced to retire. One hundred miles off the southeast coast of Japan, the fight was on but the numbers were stacked against them.

Red Leader and his wingman had been suckered by two low flying MiGs. Coming out of the sun and from the rear, Red Leader made a high-speed diving attack. Smoke erupted from the enemy MiG just as Red Leader's missile approach warning system—MAW—sounded.

Red Leader pulled hard left and deployed countermeasures to interrupt the incoming missile's tracking. He fired the chaff, a radar countermeasure in which a targeted aircraft discharges a cloud of small thin pieces of aluminum, metalized glass fiber or plastic to confuse the radar. The missile exploded close enough for the skin of Red Leader's jacket to be puckered by shrapnel.

His wingman shouted, "Red Leader, brake right, brake right!" Another missile slid past him as Red Leader started to climb, then just short of a stall, applied full rudder and yawed his airplane around facing down toward enemy aircraft. Red Leader went to guns and sent 20mm rounds smacking into and through the cockpit killing the enemy pilot.

Then Red Leader's plane disintegrated as rounds from both of his pursuers caught up with it.

Outnumbered, the Mid-Wake fighters dropped eight Russian MiGs and several of the KI before the last Mid-Wake fighter was blown out of the sky.

The first engagement of the new war, The Battle of the Sea of Japan, went to the enemy. Incredibly an order from the President of the United States himself, Phillip Greene, had prevented planes from Honolulu and the continental U.S. from being launched.

The United States of America, New Germany, and Australia had been taken out of the fight politically. The air forces of England and Spain were decimated within minutes. The KI technology was more advanced than anything the English and Spanish pilots had ever seen but it was the sheer number of Russian and KI aircraft that won the day.

It seemed that the KI craft and their pilots could not contend with the massive atmospheric disturbances with lightning along the Alaskan coastline. The flight disappeared with no survivors.

*****

General Thorne and his attack team were hiding in the boiling clouds just inland from the coast of Alaska. "Red Leader to Overlord, over."

Thorne keyed his mic, "Go ahead, Red Leader, over."

"Check your scope, Overlord, we have bogies inbound. Over."

"Overlord to Red and Blue Leaders, okay Gentlemen... You have the element of surprise and superior technology. Take them down, I re-peat...Take them down. Remember, if you can safely disable or capture at least one of the KI or one of the Russian birds… do it but the operative phrase is 'safely.' We need some Intel and we are the only ones that can get it. Over.

"Mid-Wake launched six and they did a great job but they all got splashed. No other fighters were launched from U.S. forces. Red Leader, I want you to watch for stragglers from the KI force; Blue Leader, same for you and the Russians. We need Intel, folks. Overlord, out."

Thorne maintained his overwatch position as The Egg formation divided and became Red and Blue Flights; Commander Landon Billingsly moved to engage the Russian fighters. His was outnumbered three to one but as Thorne had reminded him, "We have the element of surprise and superior technology."

Billingsly keyed his mic. "Blue Leader to Spike, you and Stormy come in low and from the right. Mase and I will come at from the high left… watch your sixes."

As Blue Leader and the Element Leader, Lieutenant Tim Carlton, fired on the Russian formation, Blue Wingman, Lieutenant Commander Mason Johnson, and Air Force Captain Hank Storm, enveloped the two halves of the formation in their own cloaking fields.

That effectively shut off the Russian's radio communication and killed their radar signatures. Billingsly's first pass dropped the odds significantly; he splashed six MiGs before they knew they were under attack and two more almost immediately.

Lieutenant Carlton's target either sensed or saw the initial attack and reacted by diving to the right. Unfortunately, that broke his flight directly into the blasts from Carlton's energy cannon.

Only six Russians survived that initial destruction and all of them attacked Carlton. Thorne keyed his mic and shouted, "I've got them, Stormy you and Mase keep the cloak around them… I've got these guys!"

Mentally, Thorne directed his energy cannons to blast. In a blistering dive, he blasted his way through the six MiGs attacking Carlton, peeled hard left and engaged the last flight of Russians. Billingsly announced his presence over the radio and he and Thorne cleaned up the last of the Russian MiGs.

Captain Hank Storm radioed, "Stormy to Overlord, Sir, I have two stragglers locked in the cloaking field… awaiting your orders."

"Overlord to Stormy, Roger that. Good job. Spike and Stormy, I want you two to double cover the Ruskies with your cloaking fields and take them to Pyramid Base. Red Leader I want you and Mase to link up on me. We're going to go give Akiro and his team a hand with the KI."

Chapter Eleven

The massive dark storm clouds now covered an area stretched from around what used to be White Horse, Yukon Territory in Canada, to well above the glaciated remains of Anchorage, Alaska. One of four formations of KI fighters were approaching from the southwest.

Two other KI formations had moved to the Mediterranean where they could impact southern Europe and Africa. The last had moved to the Pacific to control Mid-Wake, Australia and the other islands.

Red Leader, Akiro Kuriname, watched the holographic display and keyed his mic, "Red Leader to Scarecrow, over." His wingman, Lieutenant Commander Tim Hays, responded.

"Go ahead, Red Leader, over."

"Scarecrow, we have bogies coming in…"

"I see 'em, Red Leader… how do you want to play it, over?"

"Scarecrow, you and I will lock them up in our cloaks. That will leave Mad Dawg and Bowser to attack. Do you copy Mad Dawg and Bowser, over?"

"Mad Dawg to Red Leader, Roger that Sir… Bowser and I are on it. Over."

"Overlord to Red Leader, over."

"Red Leader… Overlord, over."

"Overlord to Red Leader, mind if Spike and Mase and I join in, over?"

"Red Leader to Overlord, glad to have you, Sir. Looks like there is enough to go around, over."

"Overlord to Red Leader, roger that. Looks like we captured a couple of the Russians, let's see if we can do that well with these jokers. Over."

Suddenly the direction of flight for the KI fighters changed and changed as if all of the fighters were connected to one mind and one set of controls. General Thorne saw the maneuver and said under his breath, "Maybe you boys have gotten better."

"Overlord to Red Leader, do not engage until they are in the clouds and make sure we have the cloaking devices working and the fields surround the entire formation. We don't want our surprise to get out too early. Over."

Red Leader keyed his mic, "Holy crap," he said softly. "Look at them, there's twice as many of them as us, at least."

Thorne keyed his mic, "Stow it Red Leader, we have the element of surprise and we have right on our side. Overlord, over."

"Roger that, Sir, just kinda surprised me for a second there. Over."

"Okay, Red Leader... we have a job to do. Let's get to it, over."

"Attention... attention human pilots do not attack. I repeat... do NOT attack. This is the Commander of the KI fighters you are preparing to engage. We are not your enemy."

Chapter Twelve

"KI Commander, this is Brigadier General Rodney Thorne, over."

"General Thorne, we have been sent by the one known as The Keeper. You are aware of this individual? Over."

"I am. How do I know that you are telling the truth? Better come up with something pretty quick or I will order you blasted out of the sky."

"General Thorne, by this time The Keeper will be attempting to make contact with John Rourke and Dr. Rourke will be able to verify my information. In the meantime, I understand the delicacy of our situation.

"Therefore let me offer the safety of myself and my personnel as a guarantee of our non-hostile intent. Position your craft in such a manner that you could do the most damage possible to my forces. We will follow your instructions to the letter and follow you to any secure base you wish us too. Is that acceptable, General Thorne?"

Thorne thought for a moment and switched radio frequencies, "Air Command, are you getting this? Over."

"Affirmative, Overlord. Stand by, over." Three minutes went by before General Frank Sullivan ordered Thorne not to attack the KI ships unless they directly threatened Thorne's troops or mission.

"Take them to Pyramid Base like you did the Russians. I'm on my way there. Keep them secure but do not make any provocative or menacing gestures. Just stay ready to blast the bastards into atoms, if necessary."

Chapter Thirteen

For over an hour the adults involved and the Rourke/Rubenstein children had been talking; emotions were raw and the conversations… heated.

"But why… why can't we stay here with you guys?" John Paul asked.

Michael spoke, "Because it is not safe or at least for right now it is not safe."

John Michael snorted, "The entire world died and you guys survived."

Paul held up his hand. "Look, when the world died we only had six people to worry about. Me and your mom, Uncle Michael and Aunt Natalia, Dad and Sarah and, had it not be for luck and a lot of good people, we would have died along with the majority of humanity long ago and this conversation would have never happened."

Paula held up her hand. "So why is this crisis so different? Why can't we stay with you?"

John Rourke finally spoke. "After The Night of the War, Paul and I were hunting Sarah, Michael, and Annie. Then Natalia joined our little group… most of the time we were hunting them. Occasionally, we were the hunted. The Retreat, the first one, was a secret location where we could hide and survive and remember… we did not know for sure that ANY of us would wake up from the sleep.

"We can be pretty comfortable that right now the rest of the world thinks we are dead. We can be pretty comfortable that sooner or later, and probably sooner, they will learn of their mistake and then the hunt will be on with a vengeance.

"What kept us alive before the sleep was we were mobile and with the exception of the Russians we weren't being hunted except by the small groups we had confronted.

"When they realize we are still alive, every government on the planet will be trying to find us... and us includes you. Being with us increases the danger you are in substantially. Carrying the Rourke or the Rubenstein name increases the danger you are in substantially. That is what makes this time different."

"We can't be Rourke's anymore? Natalie said. "We are going to lose our names as well as our schools, our friends, our whole lives..."

Michael put his hand on his daughter's hand. "Sweetheart, you will always be a Rourke..." He looked up at the other children. "And you guys will always be Rourkes or Rubensteins, that will never change.

"We probably should not have survived The Night of the War, none of us... even with all of the preparations that Dad had done for us. We all would have died over seven centuries ago and you guys would have never been born.

"A lot of people died so that we could survive; a lot of people died so we could get the cryogenic chambers and the serum and survive. They died because they were with us. If you are with us, you are in danger.

"You may have to continue our fight and if that is the case, you still need the training we wanted you to have when we first sent you to Camp Zero. And look at what happened there and that had nothing to do with being a Rourke or a Rubenstein."

Paula shook her head. "We thought it did but... no, our names could have been Jones and Jackson and it would have still happened. But you can't just send us away, we are not disposable..." She started crying.

John wrapped his arms around his oldest child. "Look Paula... this is not fair, I agree. This should not have to happen, I agree. But it is not something we adults wanted either, but it is what it is and we have to acknowledge that. Agreed?"

Paula nodded and sniffled, the crying stopped. "But we will be alone again, like we were at Camp Zero when everything went so bad and so wrong."

"No, you won't be alone..." Otto Croenberg stood up from the back of the room and walked forward. "John, Michael, Paul... Sarah, Natalia, and Annie. I humbly submit myself as the escort, chaperon, and guardian of your children during these difficult times. I have come to know and care for each of them and I would like to think they have some degree of affection, or at least respect for me."

"Oh, Uncle Otto... you silly... You know we love you," Sarah Ann said as she took his hand.

Croenberg picked up the child and said simply, "As long as I have breath and blood, nothing will happen to any of them." He locked eyes with each adult one at a time and held it until each had nodded. The last eyes he beheld were Sarah's; there was a tear that rolled down her left cheek when she nodded.

Chapter Fourteen

Living quarters in the Retreat 2 were not luxurious by any standard. The smell of fresh paint and cut wood was still fresh when a person stepped through the door. Otto Croenberg sat at the small table in his two-room quarters. A small kitchenette and open living room and a bedroom with latrine were all there was. Meals were normally taken in the chow hall and showers were also communal.

Shelves were present on at least half of the walls in both rooms. Unused space, such as the twelve to fifteen inches below the ceiling, easily added many square feet to each unit. There were no closets in any of the basic units; clothes were hung on a rack attached to the wall.

Each bed, no bunks here, had a headboard with concealed storage spaces in it as well as drawers beneath the mattress. Need more space? Simply add more drawers under the mattress. In one corner of the living room was a floor to ceiling bookshelf about two feet wide. The bottom three shelves slid out to make a ladder to reach the higher shelves.

Desks, tables, and work areas folded down from the wall and came in all sizes and shapes. You could have a fold-down chair added if needed. One thing you didn't have to worry about was window dressings. There weren't any, although most folks improvised artwork showing the outdoors as faux windows. After a couple of weeks and a little practice, it was amazing how much room less than five hundred square feet actually could be.

It was almost 9:00 p.m. when a knock came on Otto Croenberg's door. It was John Thomas Rourke. "Hate to call so late, but do you have a minute or two?"

Otto, in his bathrobe, bowed slightly. "Certainly, come into my humble abode. Allow me." Croenberg stepped around Rourke, unhooked the wall mounted table and dropped it into place, then dropped the seats that swung out from the wall. "What can I do for you, John?"

Rourke sat a bottle of Seagram's and two glasses on the table. "Guy talk… you and me. Not to go any further, agreed?"

Otto frowned but simply said, "Agreed."

Rourke nodded and poured two glasses. "I appreciate you stepping up to be with the kids; Michael and Paul and I all appreciate it."

Otto took a sip and smiled. "My privilege, John. I have grown quite fond of the children. I find them… intriguing; I never had any of my own."

Rourke took a sip and pulled a thin dark cigar from his pocket. "Do you mind?"

Otto smiled. "Not as long as you have another…"

"Can't smoke in the caverns themselves," Rourke said, smiling. "Disrupts the cave's ecosystem, but inside these quarters it is okay since we tied the circulation/ventilation system to the filtration system."

Croenberg produced an ashtray and Rourke rolled the striker wheel on his battered Zippo to produce that blue, yellow flame and puffed. When he had the cigar going to his satisfaction, he handed the lighter to Otto and took another sip of Seagram's. "I know the children have grown fond of you, too, Otto. I believe that someone else has also… Sarah."

Croenberg said nothing but took a puff from his now lit cigar. Rourke looked at him waiting for a response. Finally, Croenberg sat the cigar in the ashtray and stood up and looked around.

He smiled and sat back down… "Not enough room in here to pace, I just realized. So, let's have at it. Has Sarah said anything to you about me?"

Rourke couldn't tell if he was fearful she had or hopeful Sarah had spoken about him.

"Nope."

"And you wish to know what? My intentions…?"

"Nope."

"What then?"

"I want to tell you something; actually several things," Rourke said, smiling. "First of all, understand that I still love Sarah and I always will. Understand also, my time with Sarah is over. Though I love her and she loves me, we cannot reclaim what was lost so long ago. Understand there was a time when I did not like you or trust you. However, we are both older and I hope somewhat wiser."

Otto held up the whiskey glass as a toast to that thought.

"You will have charge and responsibility for the majority of what I value in this world and love most in the world."

"I know," Croenberg said softly.

Rourke sat there for a long time… neither man spoke. They smoked, they drank they stared at each other. Finally, Rourke ground out the cigar, slugged back the last of the Seagram's and shook Otto's hand. He slid the bottle over to Otto's side and headed for the door. Over his shoulder, he said simply, "Good night, good talk."

"I agree," Otto said and poured another drink.

Chapter Fifteen

Russian Colonel Mikhail Sergeyevich was unaware of what had happened in the KI Armada after he had been summoned.

He did not know of the overthrow of the Captain of the KI, nor would he have cared. The KI Captain had been an irritation to Sergeyevich. As with most nationalists, the Captain had truly felt that it was the destiny of the KI to regain their rightful place as the rulers of Earth; and that he should lead them.

The Captain had made it clear to Sergeyevich that he was simply one of the Captain's underlings. But, Sergeyevich felt he only had two masters: one was his libido and the other was his commander.

Smiling he thought that Andrea von Arnstein had control of the first; never had he experienced such wanton desire and exquisite humiliation.

Andrea knew him as he had never known himself. Dynamic and diabolical as he was in the normal world, he was putty in her hands. He shook himself, moving away from these ponderings and back to the moment at hand. He had been summoned and when one was summoned that one had best be focused and alert.

Failure to be both focused and alert meant... Sergeyevich shook himself again to drive the thought away.

Straightening his tunic one last time, he raised one hand to knock on the door, but the door opened on its own.

"Come in, Colonel," a voice rasped from inside the darkened chamber.

Sergeyevich's voice squeaked, "Colonel General..." Sergeyevich swallowed and started again. "Colonel General Petrokov, how may I be of assistance?"

Colonel General Dusan Petrokov was not feeling well, in fact he felt like hell. "Sergeyevich, give me your report, and leave nothing out."

"Colonel General, all is proceeding exactly as planned."

"Really? And does 'exactly as planned' include just your mission with the KI or does it include your extracurricular activities in France?"

Suddenly, the tunic collar on Sergeyevich's uniform felt several sizes too small.

Chapter Sixteen

Natalia's sleep was troubled, she tossed and turned. Michael sat up and placed his hand on her head to check for fever; that seemed to relax her. He slid out from under the covers and went to the bathroom to urinate then headed back to bed. He had just drifted off when Natalia sat bolt upright and screamed.

Michael grabbed her and held her as she sobbed and shook. "Babe... it's alright. I've got you. It's alright." Her crying slowly stopped and the shaking subsided. "Bad dream?"

She nodded. "Old nightmare." Her voice quivered, "Have not had it in a long time."

"Want to talk about it?" Michael asked as he pushed the hair off her forehead.

She shook her head and spoke just one word, "Karamatsov!"

Chapter Seventeen

The Grand Hall stood empty, the fireplace had been lit and the heat from it was quickly clearing the chill from the room. Roderick van Arnstein opened the door and walked in, seating himself in front of the fireplace. At over six feet tall, he was a near perfect physical specimen. The plan, his plan was coming together nicely.

Just a little longer now, he thought, *just a little longer…*

"Hello, Brother…" a voice came from behind him. Andrea van Arnstein had appeared at the far end of the Grand Hall.

"You know I do not like it when you sneak up on me," Roderick said.

She smiled and slowly walked toward him. "I am sorry. I did not mean to, you must be distracted. Is everything alright?"

He stood and held out his arms. "Yes, Sister." She walked into his arms and laid her head on his shoulder.

"Are you still upset with me Mikhail?"

"It is because of Sergeyevich, not upset as much as disappointed. I do not understand why you allow yourself to be used like that."

She giggled, "It is he that is being used. Men can be lead to do anything as long as they are following their penis."

Roderick frowned and held her back at arms distance. "Do not underestimate the Russian and certainly do not underestimate his true master. His supervisors in the Russian government are nothing but bureaucrats… it is his real master that is dangerous. That one is volatile, unpredictable and dangerous; probably more than a little bit mad also."

She moved to put her head back on his chest. "Is it true his master has lived forever?"

Roderick embraced her and smiled, "Not forever but for a very long time."

"How is that possible?" she purred.

"Evil… true evil has always existed and evil often replicates itself as it did in this instance."

"How do you mean?"

"Vladmir Karamatsov was a sadistic evil bastard and was the head of the North American branch of the KGB following The Night of the War. He was married to Major Natalia Tiemerovna, who is now the wife of Michael Rourke, former President of the United States. John Thomas Rourke shot him but the wounds were not fatal.

"Sometime later, he and Karamatsov fought again. This time Major Tiemerovna decapitated Karamatsov and stopped him. But, Karamatsov had replicated himself in the personage of Colonel Nehemiah Rozhdestvenskiy who took over the KGB after Karamatsov's death. He was so power-mad he shot down the airliner carrying the surviving members of the Soviet Politburo to the U.S."

Andrea leaned back and searched her brother's face. "But how… how is Karamatsov's evil still alive today?"

"That my dear, is truly the question."

*****

Sitting alone in his office, Roderick pondered the ties between his family and the family of Peter Vale; ties that had endured for a long time.

Long ago, the grandfathers several times removed had worked together. Had it not been for the damnable introduction of the Americans into World War II, the goal of Global Unification would have been achieved back then.

Even with the introduction of the Americans and the invasion at Normandy, it had almost worked. But the foundation of the process had been laid, even if it had to be delayed for generations. The von Arnstein family had migrated away from and back to the area around Nancy, France several times over the ages.

Roderick was fond of reminding anyone within earshot, "When the Night of the War happened, even the incredibly rich paid a price for their ideology." Within the world of the von Arnsteins, it was more tied to the sheer will of the strongest von Arnstein who, at that moment, was Roderick. Roderick and Andrea had literally been "created" for their positions.

Following the Night of the War much had to be rebuilt in the world. However, the von Arnsteins simply had to survive long enough for the world to catch its breath and regain its footing. For generations, they lived and worked within an underground commune constructed in the mid-twentieth century as a bomb shelter; thirty plus years later… the bombs actually fell and the von Arnsteins were secure far below ground.

Genetics had been around and understood for a long time but the knowledge of how to map the genome and splice genes to create the perfect specimens did not exist at the time of the Night of the War. The focused goal and the undistracted time available to the von Arnsteins and their entourage developed that science over the centuries.

Physical perfection was more easily attained as was demonstrated by the mere physical appearance of Andrea and Roderick. Their stature was "perfect," their complexions were "perfect." Mental and emotional perfection, however, had been more difficult to engineer, particularly in the female specimens.

Roderick had reasoned that since it was male scientists making the determination of perfection, it was possible their own biases were skewing the results. However, after Andrea's proclivity for "adventurous" sexual promiscuity became more obvious after puberty, he had relented. She was flawed; lovely, brilliant, artistic but… flawed.

Roderick stood and paced back and forth in his office as he reviewed Peter Vale's report. Vale had been "moderately" useful in guiding the dissolution of Michael Rourke's presidency. Admittedly a master manipulator... but by Roderick's standard Vale was not only a narcissist, he was a dangerous narcissist. Vale had no savoir-faire, no ability to be adaptable and adroit. While he did have the ability to sense or know what to do in any situation, he was like the proverbial "bull in a china shop." Still, he had been useful. Now, the question became... could Vale actually make the next step?

The idiot, Phillip Greene, was simply a place holder, a pawn... and not a very good one at that. He was too weak, too bland, too banal... so lacking in originality as to be obvious and boring. Vale, while not perfect, was both vicious and relentless when necessary. And very soon it was going to be necessary.

Chapter Eighteen

Dr. Jerome Morrell, professor of archaeology and adjunct English instructor, also dabbled in crypto-archaeology, crypto-zoology and many of the more 'unconventional' theories, such as conspiracy theories.

He had been a logical participant for John Thomas Rourke's audacious fraud attempt. When Rourke had first approached Morrell, the doctor was enticed, excited and more than a little incredulous.

"You want me to do what?"

Rourke smiled. "Look, Jerry, there is no other way to make this happen. Like I said, I need your help to prove to the world that my family and Paul Rubenstein's family are dead. If I am unable to do that, we will never be safe and our plan will be for naught."

"But, why me?"

"With the exception of just a few people, no one knows of your connection to us. Your conversations with me and my people have always been at secure locations and confidential in nature. Your conversations with Steve Delervello, the Grand Archivist, have likewise been handled below the scope of anyone's radar.

"The research you two have been doing concerning the possible existence of the rumored Third Chinese City along the Sino-Russian border lends itself to this project perfectly.

"If you agree, you and a small team will leave today and be delivered to the site in question where you will remain two days before my plan is implemented. Then you will supervise everything."

Morrell thought for just a short moment, and then a gleam came to his eyes. "Alright, Dr. Rourke, I'll do it but I'll need Delervello also. I have to have someone intelligent to talk with while we are there."

*****

Morrell and Delervello, clad in Arctic Extreme Cold Weather gear, were escorted to a secured hanger where General Rodney Thorne and Akiro Kuriname waited.

Morrell grinned. "So they were real all along, he said quietly as he walked around The Egg. "UFOs, Aliens, Atlantis… all real…"

Kuriname said, "All real, Dr. Morrell, but not at all like we thought. Here, let me take your bags." Kuriname placed Morrell's and Delervello's luggage inside what appeared to be a simple shipping container. Then he closed the double doors on the 10' x 20' x 10' container that held a variety of supplies and medical equipment.

Dr. Henry Drake, Chief of Medicine at Tripler, and three medical technicians had spent several days going over the medical equipment explaining its functions and operations.

Now it would be up to Morrell and Delervello to make everything work correctly in what would be the biggest game of legerdemain in the history of America. Not really magic, but they would be assisting in sleight of hand, skill or adroitness that had never been attempted before.

"Come on," Thorne said as he waved for them to board The Egg. "We're burnin' daylight."

Chapter Nineteen

Additional seats had been added inside The Egg and the space was more limited than normal now that there were four passengers. Kuriname monitored the tractor beam and cloaking device that would surround The Egg and the container, keeping them both invisible.

The Egg lifted off and hovered twenty or so feet in the air as the tractor beam was adjusted and raised the container several feet off the landing pad. Then both disappeared as they exited the hanger and started a climb for altitude.

Wow, Morrell thought. *Here I am actually in a UFO.*

The weather was still troubled over Alaska as they neared the Mount Denali location. On the viewscreen, it appeared they were diving toward the ground and would crash, when suddenly an opening appeared in a cliff face that had an overhang and they were flying down a tunnel. Whereas the first fifty feet appeared to be weathered rock, soon they were in a shiny metal tunnel almost forty feet across and half that distance tall.

They landed and walked to a junction where several large doors were evident. As they approached one, it silently slid up and a creature stepped out.

Morrell assessed the creature. *Elongated body and a small chest... legs shorter than what one would expect in a human, the humeri and the thighs appeared to the same length as the forearms and shins... no visible sexual characteristics...*

Head, unusually large in proportion to the body... no hair visible anywhere on the body, including the face... no noticeable outer ears or nose, only small openings or orifices for ears and nostrils... mouth small... opaque black eyes, very large but with no discernible iris or pupil... about four feet tall, maybe slightly more but only by an inch or two... My God, I am looking at a real alien.

Morrell determined the creature's lack of expression was... disconcerting. The only movement was the head which periodically moved from side to side; on a human, it could have been interpreted as quizzical or thoughtful. Slowly it stepped forward; in its right hand was a silver metal headband which he handed to Morrell.

Delervello spoke, "Rourke told me about this headband, put it on your head but sit down. His said the first connection is both painful and hits you with a little vertigo."

Morrell did as Delervello suggested, immediately his face pinched with pain. Gradually his face relaxed and he opened his eyes. "Hello," he said to the creature.

Hello... welcome... are... you... ready... to... begin? Follow... me.

Chapter Twenty

They followed the creature known as The Creator to a room that contained seventeen cubicles. In each was a variety of medical devices which could best be described as looking like a large incubator for a newborn child.

Morrell moved to the observation port and recoiled back suddenly. "My God, there are bodies in here... decapitated mutilated bodies that are breathing."

No... not... bodies... samples. Samples... that... must... be... grown... to... help... John... Rourke... with... what... you... would... call... cloned... tissue.

Akiro stepped forward. "Jerome Morrell, I take it John Rourke did not fully brief you on your mission. That is how secret this mission is. No one could know about it before it is completed and now that we have a scheduled date, everything you see must be taken to the final place for implementation. What you gentlemen are looking at is cloned tissues from each of the Rourkes and Rubensteins and a couple of other individuals."

Morrell was still shocked. "But they are human bodies..."

"No... No, they aren't, at least not in the normal sense," Kuriname said. "There is no mind, no soul...simply living but non-sentient tissue grown in a laboratory from stem cell samples taken from the host and genetically modified to only produce what you see before you.

"All of the samples were donated except two which was obtained secretly from the host or parent human; you and Mr. Delervello. Animated but non-sentient tissue samples that will give the Rourkes and the Rubensteins anonymity for the next phase of the operation."

*****

Two days before the explosion that "killed" the Rourkes and Rubensteins, the thirteen "tissue samples" were transported.

On the night of the explosion, after the Rourkes and Rubensteins and their children had left the residence by way of the beach, Jerry Morrell and Steve Delervello had carefully laid each of the samples in the appropriate beds in the appropriate rooms. Then they evacuated via the beach where they were picked up by a fishing boat registered to Air Force Chief of Staff, Frank Sullivan.

This was the same boat that had picked up the Rourkes and Rubensteins almost four hours earlier.

After the explosions, the "remains" of the Rourkes and Rubensteins and their children had been recovered. There was barely enough to identify each victim, but there was enough.

Funerals for the victims were held at one time with cremations that followed. That included three unidentified bodies assumed to be friends or colleagues of the Rourkes.

Eventually, one of those bodies would be identified as belonging to Dr. Jerome Morrell, a professor of archaeology and an adjunct English instructor.

Another body would be determined to be that of Mr. Steve Delervello who occupied the position of Grand Archivist of the Mid-Wake Institute.

Chapter Twenty-One

In the days following the death of the Rourkes and Rubensteins and following the inauguration of President Phillip Greene, there was a scramble going on. While the forces under President Greene scrambled to consolidate their power, others were scrambling to build camouflage that might protect them and their mission.

William Robert "Beaux Diddley" Delys, P.I. from Baton Rouge and ex-HPD cop had just returned from Europe where he, Tuviah Friedman and Otto Croenberg had been investigating the power behind the New World Order threat. Delys had heard of the explosion that killed the Rourkes and Rubensteins on the morning news as most of Hawaii did.

His phone rang. "Have you been watching this news?"

Delys recognized Tuviah's voice. "I have."

"Then it has begun?"

"It has." The connection was broken. Twenty minutes later, Delys walked out of his rented condo with two suitcases and a small overnight bag. As he stepped into the street and headed toward his car, he spotted two men watching him and trying very hard not to be seen watching him.

Okay, he thought. *I guess it really has begun.* Entering the parking garage, he approached his car and realized the piece of clear tape he had placed to stick to both the fender and the hood of the car was missing.

He kept walking as sweat broke out on his upper lip. *Damn, this ain't good,* he thought. *I've got to get out of this garage.*

Each level of the garage had both an elevator and a stairwell door that connected that level to stairs and emptied out into the shopping mall next door. He opened the door and closed and locked it behind him. He unzipped one suitcase, removed a light jacket and a baseball cap. He zipped the luggage closed and sent it sliding down to the next level along with the other suitcase.

Putting on the light jacket and ball cap he took the magazines, extra ammo, and flashlight out of the overnight bag and shoved it in the trash receptacle and headed up to the next level. He was now on the run.

Chapter Twenty-Two

Delys walked quickly but confidently through the third floor of the shopping mall past a clothing store and a food court. He entered a service elevator, scanning behind to try and catch watching eyes and seeing none, he pushed the button for the basement. When the doors opened, he hesitated long enough to make sure he wasn't walking into a trap. Picking the lock to the power equipment room, he slipped inside.

Having scouted this escape route a month ago, he knew that one of the ventilation ducts serviced both this building and the one next door. He climbed atop one of the service panels and pried open the duct cover. After he was in, he pulled the cover shut and quietly crawled through the ductwork.

Arriving at the other end, he sat for several minutes to ensure the room was empty, popped the cover and dropped to the floor. He slowly opened the door and peered outside, seeing nothing he walked quickly down the hall, up one flight of stairs and out into the street. Watching in the store windows and using them like mirrors, he observed the street around him as he looked for someone tailing him. He saw nothing.

He crossed the street against the light hoping to pick out someone trying to follow him; he saw no one. He saw nothing. He saw nothing as the van slammed into him as he crossed the second street. He felt nothing as the impact threw him forward ahead of the van. He felt nothing as the right side wheels rolled over him. He saw nothing as he stopped rolling and lay still on his back.

He did not even see the man that spoke into the microphone hidden in his hand and kept walking down the other side of the street.

Chapter Twenty-Three

After the KI commander had made contact, Kuriname and his flight elements escorted the KI to the secret Alien complex near Mount Denali in what was formerly Alaska.

This was the complex that John Thomas Rourke had been rescued from; it was the complex of the alien known as The Creator.

Akiro Kuriname and General Rodney Thorne sat across from the commander of the KI fighter group. He was tall, over six feet tall with strong chiseled features and short cut stubble on his scalp and the posture of a military professional. He appeared to have slightly oriental facial characteristics. Like the others, he wore a jumpsuit of a silvery, metallic appearing cloth.

As close as they could figure, his rank was similar to a Commander in Earth forces. Like The Keeper, the commander's name was not pronounceable in the English language.

To Kuriname's Element Leader, Lieutenant Layne "Mad Dawg" Washington, it had sounded something like Crenshaw. That had sounded agreeable to the commander so it stuck.

"Crenshaw" was stoic as any member of the KI that Kuriname had met, but... "Crenshaw" almost had a sense of humor... almost. Having the KI surrender the Russian side arms they were armed with, "Crenshaw"—who stood head and shoulders over the humans—had simply smiled as he looked down at them.

Kuriname had put on the headband and mentally requested an audience with The Creator.

Moments later, The Creator stepped through one of the sliding doors into the section of the outer tunnels that had been assigned to the humans.

Using the headband by which The Creator and John Rourke had communicated was both uncomfortable and painful for Kuriname to learn to use, but Rourke had insisted that communication and coordination must be continued with The Creator.

Why… are… the… Others… here?

Kuriname said, "They are here to help us."

The creature known as The Creator had been briefed but was obviously not pleased with the circumstances. The Creator spun and unceremoniously walked out of the sliding door.

Before long the section in the outer tunnels soon included a Command Center, small kitchen and bunks. The hanger section now contained the nine Egg craft flown by Thorne and his team, and twenty-two KI fighters newly added by the KI commander.

The Creator appeared again and Kuriname put the headband back on. Does… Rourke… approve… of… this?

Kuriname said, "I have not spoken directly to Rourke but he is aware of these new developments."

Can… not… trust… the… Others.

"I know of one that can be trusted and he is the one that sent these here. He is the one we call The Keeper."

Rourke… trusts… him.

"He does and I do as well."

The Creator turned and left. Kuriname did not know if that was or was not a good thing.

The KI known as "Crenshaw" smiled slightly. "So THAT is what I have heard about all of my life as the ENEMY that destroyed our world and forced us into space? With one hand I could crush its skinny neck."

Kuriname cut his eyes to the KI, "Being able to does not mean you should or you will, Commander. Do I make myself clear?"

Commander "Crenshaw" smiled. "As you humans would say, 'Would that I could but I can't,' is that the expression?"

Kuriname said, smiling, "It is close enough."

"Would that I could but I can't," the KI Commander chuckled. "Maybe it should be changed to, 'Because I can I should?'"

Kuriname smiled. "Better leave it at, 'I know you can and you could but I wouldn't if I were you.'"

"Why would I not if I can?"

"Because I know The Keeper and he would not be pleased and I can't see you taking any pleasure in defeating a foe so much smaller than yourself. Do you know the concept of sportsmanship? A big person like you defeating a smaller being like The Creator; there would be no glory in that."

"Crenshaw" interlaced his fingers forming a steeple then reversed his hands, palms out and pushed, cracking his knuckles loudly and smiled. "Maybe no glory but much satisfaction."

He sat upright and smiled again. "Do you know that I am the only person of my people that has been that close to someone from his people in 40,000 of your years?"

He cracked his knuckles again and smiled. "Now what is that expression again... oh, yes... 'How near and yet how far.'"

He looked at the door The Creator had exited through. "How near and yet how far..."

Chapter Twenty-Four

Peter Vale stood at the edge of the viewing glass for the Aquarium in downtown Honolulu. A disguised Phillip Greene had managed to ditch his Secret Service detail and stood near enough to hear Vale's whispered responses as he asked, "How is the project going?"

Vale laughed softly. "Project… the project is going well. Anyone in the government or military that is thought to be loyal to Michael Rourke has been compartmentalized… which means every form of potential communication between that person and any other Rourke loyalists can now be intercepted and studied.

"Minor players without any particular value or power in an obvious sense have been simply eliminated. So far, no one seems upset by these accidents or even knowledgeable of them. A lot of dissimilar accidents and individual tragedies have not made an observable pattern as of yet. What are you hearing from the other heads of state, Mr. President?"

Greene cleared his throat and dabbed at the corner of his mouth with a handkerchief. "As you know America, Australia, and New Germany have given permission for occupying Russian and KI forces to be landed. After the initial battles with England and Spain that wiped out their air forces, land and naval forces were activated to repulse invaders. Those forces were decimated in less than a day and now all that remains is weak, civilian and partisan resistance."

Vale watched a shark that swam lazily into view. "Any word on the missing KI fighters?"

Greene subconsciously shook his head. "They were probably destroyed by the intense storms over the Alaskan coast and northwestern Canada but we can't be sure. No issue anyway, really."

"And how are we doing on the world-wide summit? When will that take place?"

"I have contacted the other heads of state and explained the need for not only having the meeting but handling it quickly. Frankly, since America, Australia and New Germany are the only major countries that still have a standing military... well, not to mention Russia of course, there is really no one to stand against us, is there?"

Vale smiled. "That Mr. President was the plan all along."

Chapter Twenty-Five

John Thomas Rourke, Paul Rubenstein, and Michael Rourke sat in the main dining hall of the Retreat 2, alone... alone with a map of the world. John finally spoke, "Well, the Golden Age of Philosophy was in ancient Greece."

"I don't see how that makes things any brighter," Paul said. "The whole world is about to fall under communism and the New World Order."

"Dad, is this how it felt back then, in the early days right after The Night of the War?" Michael asked.

Rourke was smoking a thin dark cigar that had just gone out. He pulled the battered Zippo from his pocket and relit it with a couple of puffs. "Pretty much, Michael... Everything seemed doomed, everything seemed over. There was little hope of anything good coming from the destruction."

"How did you and Paul go on?"

Paul Rubenstein turned to Michael. "When you and Annie were older, after the first sleep... you fought. You experienced the fear of fear, the dread of dread... the hopelessness and you didn't quit."

John added, "There is always a hope because freedom is the natural condition of mankind, an English guy named Thomas Hobbes said that in the Seventeenth Century. Oh, kings and despots arise from time to time to enslave man, but men rebel against that slavery. We saw it back in the old days.

"We fought with people who were willing to die for freedom, if not their own, then someone else's; if not the freedom of their bodies, then the freedom of their will. Resistance fighters, guerrilla fighters have always had an advantage over a standing army; all the way back to Robin

Hood and William Wallace and Geronimo and the French Marque during World War II.

"Hobbes argued that all humans are by nature equal in faculties of body and mind and no one 'should have any claim to an exclusive benefit' over other men. It was one of the founding principles of America, seems so simple, so true but oh so hard to remember."

"So what do we do?"

Rourke said, smiling, "There was a Marine General named "Chesty" Puller who was once surrounded by the enemy. He declared, 'All right, they're on our left, they're on our right, they're in front of us, they're behind us... they can't get away this time. Great, now we can shoot at those bastards from every direction."

"But, John, these 'bastards' outnumbered us," Paul said.

"But how many times did we face a larger force than you and me and we prevailed; ever wonder how that worked?" John asked.

"Sure, but I'm more concerned how it will work in these circumstances."

"There is an old adage, 'When a small force is in a battle where the only salvation is fighting without delay; that is death ground.' The Allies faced that on D-Day; the majority of troops that landed that day were not seasoned soldiers but raw troops who knew they could die and would die, if they didn't fight... so they fought and they won."

"That's not much of a battle plan..." Michael said.

"It's the only one we've got," John replied.

Chapter Twenty-Six

Sarah was preparing for bed when she heard a knock on her cabin door. Looking at her watch and seeing the time, she became concerned. Slipping a robe on over her lingerie she said, "Coming, I'm coming."

Otto Croenberg stood at her door. "I apologize for the lateness of the hour but it is important that I speak to you. May I come in?" Sarah stood back and Croenberg stepped in. "Thank you for this opportunity, Sarah. I need to speak with you."

Sarah nodded. "You said that already, Otto. What do we need to speak about?"

Croenberg had that "deer in the headlight look"; he suddenly realized that he had no idea what he was going to say to this woman. After all of the conversations he had played in his head, he had no idea what he was going to say to her.

While he had some hopes for how she felt, some dreams about how he wanted her to feel… those words had never been spoken except in his mind.

Sarah saw it in his face. "Otto, what has happened?"

Croenberg stammered for a moment before getting it out, "I spoke with John."

"Okay…"

"Actually, John spoke with me."

"Okay…" Sarah waited and finally asked, "What did you and John talk about?"

"Uh, you. About what we should do."

"What we should do about what, Otto?" she asked with a smile.

"The children..."

"Who's children… what are you talking about?"

"John's, Paul's and Michael's children…" Sarah waited. "John told me I will have charge and responsibility for the majority of what he values in this world and loves most in the world."

"And you said?"

"I said, 'I know,'" Croenberg said softly.

"And John said?"

"He said, 'Good night, good talk.'"

"John said, 'Good night, good talk?'"

Otto nodded, Sarah kissed him on the lips and escorted him to the door and opened it. "Then I will say good talk and good night, also."

Otto Croenberg, former assassin, former Neo-Nazi, former President of the Democratic Republic of Germany stood outside the door as it closed, sweating. He could still feel the kiss.

Chapter Twenty-Seven

Much of war is often resolved in the first six months. Occupation forces take control, governments are modified and things settle into something called "a new normal." Lives are lost, property is destroyed. Gradually, services return and the "normal" activities of society return. Electricity is turned back on, water is restored, babies are born and hospitals reopen and not everyone is dying because of the war.

At least, this is the plan for a "civilized war." You see in civilized war, destruction is no longer necessary; complacency has replaced it. There are, however, those rare folks that refuse complacency and refuse to comply.

Dr. David Blackman, Chief of Psychological Research at Mid-Wake, was checking in on his newest indigent patient, Emily Sheppard. Ms. Sheppard was a widow who had lost her family in the plague caused by the VBB, the Very Bad Bug. This was a manmade genetic aberration that had killed thousands.

Ms. Sheppard was suffering from a dissociative fugue with one or more episodes of amnesia in which an individual cannot recall some or all of his or her past. Either the loss of one's identity or the formation of a new identity may occur with sudden, unexpected, purposeful travel away from home. Ms. Sheppard's symptoms had recently manifested with a severity that had required hospitalization.

She smiled when she saw Dr. Blackman at the door of her room. "Doctor, it is nice to see you again."

"Hello, Emily," Blackman said as he entered. "How are you doing today?"

"I'm actually quite well; I think I am ready to go home."

"I have someone that would like to see you, may I bring him in?"

"Certainly," she said, smiling.

Blackman reached back and pushed the door open and nodded. A rumpled man with a five o'clock shadow entered. "Emily, this is a friend of mine named Tim. His daughter is one of my former patients."

"Hello, Tim. I'm Emily, Emily Sheppard."

"Pleased to meet you, Ms. Sheppard," he said, shaking her outstretched hand. It seemed to Emily he held it a bit longer than appropriate. She frowned and pulled away. Tim smiled and said, "Forgive me, Ms. Sheppard, it is just you remind me of my daughter."

"Is she a patient here?" Emily asked, now smiling.

"No, she's lost I'm afraid," he said, turning to Blackman. "Thank you, Doctor, but I must go now."

"Of course, let me walk you out," Blackman said.

"Nice to meet you, Ms. Sheppard," Tim said.

Chapter Twenty-Eight

John stood watching as Sarah walked down the hill toward him. He pointed over his shoulder. "This is what's left of the Little Sac River, and it's one of nine tributaries in the Sac River Basin."

Sarah sat down on a rock ledge. "I doubt you wanted to talk to me about the river."

John sat down and reached for her hand and when she took his, he smiled. "Who would have ever thought our lives would turn out like they have, Sarah?"

Sarah smiled. "Well, I could not have foreseen the specific twists and turns but I think we both realized there was something else God had in store for us. John, you know I'll always love you, right?"

Smiling, he squeezed her hand. "Just as I will always love you, Sarah. I wish…"

Sarah Rourke-Mann put her hand to his lips. "Don't say it, John. Things turned out the way they turned out; that's all. For a while… a beautiful while, you had a wonderful life with Emma and I had the same with Wolfgang. You may still be able to recover that life with Emma. I can never get Wolf back. The good news is we still love and respect each other, even if we both know we could never live together." She smiled and with a laugh said, "I'd probably kill you myself."

John smiled. "I know and you probably should have long ago." He grew serious, "I'm worried, Sarah, I'm worried about you and the kids and I'm worried about the world."

This time she squeezed his hand. "So am I, John. So am I. But once, a long time ago… when this all started, I took two children and a couple of horses and survived until you found us. Over the years I've gotten pretty good at surviving myself."

"You have at that. I'm proud of you."

Sarah frowned. "I want to say this carefully, John. I don't... I truly don't want to hurt you... but what is most important to me is I am proud of myself. It has been a long time since I sat in your shadow. I appreciate what you say, but what I think and how I feel are more important to me. Please don't take this wrong, I do love you."

He smiled and stood, still holding her hand. "I understand what you mean and I agree and again... I am proud of you and I love you, too." He leaned down and gently kissed her forehead. "I wish you good luck and God's speed and I will never not be there for you." He turned to leave.

She held his hand and smiled. "And I will never not be there for you, but now we must find our own selves and be..."

He finished her thought, "... and be what we can become."

She watched him walk out of her life again and wondered if it would be for the last time.

Chapter Twenty-Nine

"She had no idea who I am, did she, Doctor?"

"No, Mr. Shaw… she did not."

"But she was normal, well not normal but just depressed after the death of the baby. Why now is it she doesn't know who she is or me for that matter?"

"When we decided it would be best to 'hide' your daughter while she was getting treatment for the stress and depression, we knew there was some degree of risk. We thought having her here at Mid-Wake would be best; particularly since we could keep her true identity a secret.

"The bad news is apparently the added stress in shifting her location and circumstances exacerbated her condition and pushed her into something resembling an amnesic shift with a newly assumed personality. The good news is I still believe this is a temporary condition."

Tim Shaw, father of Emma Rourke, who was now known as Emily Sheppard, checked his watch. "I have to leave now if I'm going to make the last flight out of Mid-Wake tonight. My forged ID is only good for fourteen more hours. I need to get back and report to John Rourke on her condition."

Blackman nodded. "Tell John that things here are secure and she is safe. The occupying forces are not interfering too much, particularly with the schools and hospitals. I'm confident she will be safe here and her identity is protected. Even she has no idea who she is and I'm one of only two people here that know her true identity."

"Thanks, Doc. Take care of my little girl."

Chapter Thirty

Tuviah Friedman was cold, the rain and fog were doing nothing to help his mood either. The days following the takeover had been filled with rumors, half-truths, and speculations. The news media outlets had been seized and were under the control of... well, that was one of the questions. Who was in control?

All the general public knew was the Russians and militant KI had joined forces and the governments of the world's countries had either capitulated or their military forces had been destroyed. To date, there had been no public statement from either the Russians or the forces of the KI Empire and that situation was entering its third week. Rumors abounded but facts were in short supply.

The organization that Tuviah worked for, the Aqrab, hunted Neo-Nazis. Or, more accurately it could be said "had" hunted Neo-Nazis. The Aqrab, which translates to "The Scorpion," had gone silent immediately after the takeover. This was not an uncommon situation for The Scorpions. Many times, circumstances had shifted or the fear that circumstances had shifted and the organization had gone silent. Their silence had twice been the only reason they had survived.

Tuviah had a feeling that somehow this time was different, though he could not articulate it. A feeling is like that... just a feeling without shape or substance. Tuviah was having another feeling right now. He had the feeling he was being followed.

The rain and fog didn't help anything, nor did it assist him in identifying who was watching him. He had stepped into the doorways of several buildings that had offered protection from the falling rain. As he lit his pipe, he looked and watched for a sign that would indicate who and where his tail was, unsuccessfully.

He smiled to himself as he lit his pipe again. The inset doorway blocked the wind and the second floor created a space where the cold rain couldn't reach him. The little man was actually warming up as he puffed on his pipe. He shook the rain from his long coat and slapped his hat against his leg in a vain attempt to rid it of rainwater.

He continued to scan the street in front of him. Several people had exited the store behind him, bumping into him and apologizing. He had chosen this store carefully to set up his observation point; it was a corner convenience store. By leaning slightly forward he could see the street in front of him and the side street beside him.

Like most corner convenience stores, it catered to the local population. He had known hundreds of them in a thousand cities across what was left of the world. They all were small stores stocking a wide variety of essential items for their clientele based on their economic and cultural needs. They often sold food and snacks that were made on-site. Those could be anything from tacos and burritos to kosher hotdogs.

What were those things Beaux Delys had given me, he tried to remember. He smiled. *He called them boudin, boudin balls with Creole mustard dipping sauce.* They were a south Louisiana specialty made from pork and rice sausage, removed from its casing, and formed into balls that are then breaded and deep-fried.

Like so many other corner convenience stores, this one sold everything from alcohol to lottery tickets… soda to coffee. He had heard them called "corner stores," "packies" and even bodegas; what you call the store on the corner says a lot about where you live.

Tuviah stepped inside and bought a cup of coffee then went back outside to stand. The rain was coming down much harder now. He watched a woman flick open her umbrella as she exited a cab and moved quickly to the doorway. She was already drenched by the time Tuviah stepped back and made room for her in the doorway.

She slipped on the wet sidewalk and Tuviah stepped forward to grab her; she was a pretty thing, he noted. Both hands had remained on the umbrella and as Tuviah grabbed her around the waist, the umbrella separated at the handle.

Tuviah caught the scent of her perfume, the softness of her long hair brushed his cheek as he caught her; she was lovely and smelled of lilac. With her left hand she shifted the canopy over Tuviah's shoulder and back, effectively blocking the vision of anyone inside the bodega.

She smiled prettily at Tuviah as her right hand moved quickly. The eight-inch spike blade that had been secreted in the umbrella handle slid into Tuviah just below his solar plexus and plunged smoothly upward... upward into his heart. Still smiling, she said, "Thank you, Sir."

Stepping back, the spike slid silently back into the handle and she walked quickly away. Tuviah stood leaning against the side of the doorway. It had happened so quickly, so expertly, his body had not yet registered the event... but his mind had; almost. Through the haze of his pain, he heard his father say, "Ben shelí, my son..."

Confused, Tuviah smiled. "Abba... is it you?"

"Of course," his father smiled. "Who else would it be? Do not say that which you were about to say... do not curse. I know there is shock and surprise at the pain, but the Torah tells you that to be holy you should remember that using bad language does more than keep you from being one step above. It actually shleps you down."

Tuviah smiled as he slid down the wall. "Yes, Abba... I remem..."

Tuviah Friedman did not know he was, in fact, the last of the Scorpions as he died in the doorway of the bodega.

Chapter Thirty-One

The Grand Hall was silent and dark; then a soft, barely audible gong sounded and lights came on in the hall. Andrea von Arnstein entered through the door on the left side of the massive fireplace. A second gong sounded and from the right door entered her brother Roderick. Behind each of them, a line of people walked to their prescribed seats around the large, plain rectangular table that sat in the center of the Grand Hall. The procession was formal, almost medieval…

Andrea took her place at the foot of the table as Roderick stood at the head. Its surface was polished but the wood was ancient and worn. Around the table sat forty-nine heavy wood and leather chairs. When everyone was standing in place, Roderick nodded and they sat.

Roderick turned to his left. "Alexander, would you begin with your report?"

Alexander Corti, head of the Intelligence Committee, rose. "Operations are proceeding as successfully as anticipated. We have just received word that the last of the Aqrab agents has been successfully terminated. That should close the door on any and all potential issues with resistance. The governments of the United States, New Germany, and Australia, as well as the remaining European countries, have all signed non-aggression packs with our representatives. Effectively the Union of Earth States is a reality."

Polite applause met the announcement.

"When will we go public, Mr. Chairman?" someone asked.

Roderick turned back to Corti. "Alexander?"

Corti smiled. "Mr. Chairman… as there are no further holdouts from the world governments and since our Russian allies and our supporters from the KI Empire have solidified our positions and control... That decision is yours to make."

Roderick looked at Andrea and smiled. She nodded and said, "Let us go around the table and listen to all of the reports before we finalize that decision." From around the table reports of finance, transportation, economics and logistics and every other constituent part of taking over the entire planet were voiced.

All save one.

Roderick called on Demetrius Conte, head of the Continuity Committee, "Demetrius, what is your input?"

Conte cleared his throat. "Mr. Chairman, as you know... we sit on the precipice of something utterly remarkable in the course of human history; all of the nations of the world operating under the guidance and control of one group. While it has been tried before... it has never moved to this level of accomplishment.

"As I have said before, control is hard won and easily lost. Logic is essential when dealing with affairs of state but it has a way of disintegrating when it comes to the hearts and minds of citizens. Our current endeavors trace their history back to the activities of Pope Gregory IX in the middle ages and his discriminatory dictates. Throughout history, the Jewish people have led a precarious existence and were condemned to a status of perpetual servitude by Church doctrine and imperial decree and often confined to narrow, unhealthy ghettos.

"But they have also served as scapegoats throughout history when it was necessary for outbreaks of mob violence. We have a long line of precedence for blaming the Jews for anything that requires someone to be blamed for. I see nothing of concern there.

"The logic and benefits of our dominance and control cannot be argued except by those who we shall dominate and control. As I have said before, we must maintain dominance and control for a period of at least two generations if we are to be successful. We must breed out of exist-ence all concepts of the individual… of individual rights and thought and speech.

"Shortly we shall have taken over the world, now we must entertain the world's citizens. We must ensure good breweries, lovely beaches, and lovely women. We have already identified the first of those 'strong men and women' who will deal directly with the people. We must cycle them out periodically to keep the citizens unbalanced while being enter-tained. This is no more difficult than what the Roman Empire did with the Coliseum and the gladiators.

"We have already secured our funding; ergo there is no issue there. Branding our product will be an ongoing public relations campaign that is positive as well as entertaining. Most people, who have a full belly and have their lust satisfied, will languish forever in a slavery that no one tells them about.

"Our standing military forces must gradually become more benign. But that is only after the worst of the resistance is dealt with brutally and finally. No mercy and no quarter can be given, only extermination. We must approach and seduce the children and press them into service and reward them with all they need to be 'successful.'

"When you control the media, you control the dinner table and the conversations that take place around it. When you control the schools and universities, you can outwait the dissidents. You don't have to fight and kill them, you just let them die off from old age and stupidity. When you control the police and the courts, laws can be easily created to facilitate any action necessary. When you control the banks and com-merce, you control the consumables and the consumption of all things, and who gets to consume what.

"In short order you will see that the citizenry will continue on with "business as usual." In other words, a new normal will be created. As long as turmoil is planned and choreographed and kept from the affected everyday citizen, they will worship their own lack of control. There will still be wars... wars are necessary for mankind. We will simply control those wars. When necessary we will use them to put down rebellion or, on occasion, to start proxy rebellions that benefit us.

"This has been going on for years and the citizens of the world were simply too stupid to understand what was happening. We must actually do some nation building, particularly in those undeveloped countries that never regained their status from before The Night of the War. We must possess more than just repressive secret police and brutal military. After all, we are now the World Bank and commerce is the real secret of control of the masses. We must generate Gross Domestic Products.

"Some of those, of course, will continue to be poppies and coca leaves and meth and other 'drugs of choice.' The most difficult citizens to control are those that are healthy. Drug addicts make very positive contributions to society. They will do anything for their drugs and they show the majority of society how good the majority actually has it. There is, however, one thing we must avoid."

"And what is that?" Andrea asked.

Demetrius Conte, head of the Continuity Committee, said smiling, "We must never bask in our victory. We must never let our guard down, we must both live up to and down to the expectations of the people we rule. After all, taking over an entire world is hard work."

Chapter Thirty-Two

Russian Army Colonel General Anatoly Ivanov, was a history buff and somewhat of an anachronism.

For example, he had graduated first in his class at the Malinovsky Military Armored Forces Academy, named after Marshal Rodion Malinovsky. Its mission was to train Russian commanders, staff officers and engineers for armored and mechanized units before the Night of the War.

He had won a position that he still maintained as an adjutant Epee fencing coach at the academy. He also had studied painting at the Russian Academy of Arts or the Repovsky Institute as it was also known.

His favorite period of history was just before the Night of the War. He had studied all of the military data that had survived and had recently been gifted a set of books by an American author named Paul Rubenstein. These were called *The Rourke Chronicles* and told the story of Rubenstein and Doctor John Thomas Rourke's adventures immediately after the opening of hostilities. Ivanov found them particularly intriguing as they were the first accounts he had seen of the war from the American side.

Of particular interest to him were accounts of one of his personal heroes, General Ishmael Varakov. He had studied Varakov's actions during World War II and the years preceding The Night of the War, but Rubenstein's impressions of him were particularly interesting.

Ivanov regretted he would never get to discuss Varakov with Rubenstein as he had died during the explosion that killed Rourke, his son Michael who was President of the United States, and their families. He had just finished volume one of the Chronicles entitled *Everyman* and started volume two, *Demons and Monsters* when he heard about the explosion. He had lamented to his staff that day, "What a loss to mankind… those people witnessed the end of their world and now have joined it. What a loss…"

Ivanov checked his wall clock; it was time for Colonel Mikhail Sergeyevich's appointment. Ivanov was neither amused nor enthused by the prospect; he found Sergeyevich… unseemly.

A knock came at the office door and his orderly announced the Colonel's presence. "Send me him." Sergeyevich marched in the room, ramrod straight… eyes forward and stopped exactly two feet from the desk and centered on it."

Ivanov noted the precision; he had never mastered it himself. Sergeyevich saluted and Ivanov delayed an imperceptible second before returning the salute. He recognized it in his own mind as simply a note of power to subjugate the arrogant Colonel, and then he called him by his first name… not in comradery but again from a position of power.

"Well, Mikhail, what news do you have for me?"

"Colonel General, I am pleased to announce all is proceeding as directed." Sergeyevich was braced at parade rest, still ramrod straight and eyes forward. "Our Russian forces along with our KI allies rendered both the British and Spanish governments non-existent and our forces are consolidating positions of strength throughout the rest of the world. We expect…"

"Who is 'we,' Mikhail?"

Sergeyevich blinked several times in rapid succession, knocked off his stride. "We… by we, Colonel General, I mean my superiors."

Ivanov smiled. "So you mean your superiors expect what, Mikhail?"

"Total control by the end of the week, Colonel General."

Ivanov leaned forward. "Mikhail, I am hearing rumors of 'other players' in this game."

Sergeyevich blinked again. "Sir?"

"That is what I am asking you, Mikhail; is there anything I should know but do not?"

Sergeyevich's blinking became intense. *How much does the bastard know and what does he know and how does he know it?* "Not that I am aware of Colonel General."

"Good, Mikhail, it would be… unseemly, if you had information I did not possess."

Chapter Thirty-Three

The morning sun was just breaking, rays of light stabbing through the overcast sky above Retreat 2. The escort vehicles were ready and manned.

Had someone been watching from above, the small clusters of people would have seemed sad.

John Thomas Rourke sat on a rock just outside the main cavern.

Paula, John and Emma Rourke's oldest child, was now almost eighteen and almost a woman. Her brother, Timothy, now almost sixteen was looking more and more like his father and becoming taciturn like his father.

Rourke's eldest son, Michael, stood with his wife Natalia and their children, John Paul, nearing fifteen and Sarah Ann who was trying to act older than her mere ten years of age.

Paul and Annie were trying to console John Michael and Natalie, who was now seventeen with a birthday coming up. John Michael like Tim and John Paul, was losing his childhood and moving into the body of a young man.

Sarah Rourke-Mann watched from the sidelines. She knew her time to interact would be when they all climbed onboard the VTOL, the Vertical Take Off and Landing transport, that would take the children and their "chaperons" to the next training school.

Next to her stood Otto Croenberg, tall and stoic. "It will be alright, Sarah," he finally said.

"I know it will be, but this… this is so hard for the kids and it is hard for their parents."

Croenberg nodded. "It is, but your presence is making it easier for all of them. You know that and how much harder it would be for the parents to let them go… especially after the attack they suffered from those damn Starlings."

Sarah turned and squeezed Croenberg's arm. "Thank you, Otto. I appreciate that."

Croenberg gave a pitiful smile and wondered, *What was that expression I heard the other day?* He heard one of the technicians describing the first time he had met John Rourke, "I was nervous as a long-tailed cat in a room full of rockin' chairs." Right now he knew exactly how that technician had felt.

One of Wes Sanderson's men came up to him and saluted. "Chief, we have all of the equipment loaded on the VTOL. We can begin loading passengers when you are ready."

Sanderson returned the salute and smiled. "Let's give them a few more minutes. This will be the last time for a long time for them to be together. I'll let you know when we'll start to board." The man saluted and retired to watch the tableau playing out in front of him.

John Rourke reached down and picked up a package he handed to his son, Timothy. "Son, I want you to take this with you, you might need it and it has served me very well."

Tim Rourke unwrapped the package and stared; it was the Jack Crain, LSX knife his father had carried for so long.

"I have replaced all survival items in the handle and its cord wrapping, the sheath has been saddle soaped and the blade edges resharpened."

"Paula." Rourke turned to his daughter and handed her a package. Inside was a Detonics Pocket Nine, the stainless 9mm little brother of his CombatMasters. "I don't want you to be unarmed anymore and you have always favored a 9mm."

He handed her another package. "Inside here is a copy of the belt holster and double magazine carrier made for me by Lou Alessi of the Alessi

Holster Company when I got the gun before The Night of the War. I've treated the leather on it also. Both have served me well, but I hope you never have to use either of them. Also, here are several boxes of 115 grain jacketed hollow points, Federals."

Michael and Paul Rubenstein were similarly arming their children. Sarah watched as a variety of pistols and blades she recognized changed hands; a cold chill went up her spine.

John Rourke looked over to Sanderson and gave a quick nod, it was time to go. Sanderson nodded back and waved his arm in a circle above his head. "Okay, let's saddle up."

Natalia and Annie hugged all of the kids as John, Michael and Paul prepared to ride with them to the VTOL. Paula grabbed Annie hard then pushed her back and looked hard into her eyes. "I'm counting on you to watch over Mom for me and if anything happens to her... I am going to trust you to make sure we get back to take care of her."

Annie nodded. "Don't worry. I won't let you down."

Sarah took Paula's hand and Otto Croenberg picked up Sarah Ann. "Time to go Little One."

A tear ran down Sarah Ann's face. "I know Uncle Otto... I know."

John, Michael, and Paul led the way in one of the All Terrain Powered Armored Attack Vehicles.

Sarah Ann, Otto and Sarah Rourke-Mann climbed into the first AATV to be transported to the VTOL. Paula and Natalia climbed into the next one and John Paul, John Michael and Timothy climbed into the last one.

As they passed Wes Sanderson at the gate, all three saluted. Sanderson, not usually caught by surprise, dropped his full cup of coffee and smartly returned the salute. As the vehicles passed out of his sight he murmured, "Go with God."

*****

The big VTOL cargo plane seemed larger than normal to John Rourke as he watched the kids board. Croenberg sat Sarah Ann down and she scrambled to join her brother and sister.

He and Sarah came over to the fathers as they stood together. "John, Michael, Paul… thank you for letting me do this." Sarah smiled a hard smile, "I'll watch them like a mother hawk." Her voice cracked.

"We know you will, Mom," Michael said.

"We are all just glad that you and Otto agreed to do this," Paul said. "It will just be too dangerous for them here." John Thomas Rourke placed his hands on his ex-wife's shoulders.

"I just wish Emma was here so I could tell her…" Sarah said.

Rourke smiled. "I'll tell her for you, take care of you so you can take care of them, Sarah." She nodded, gave him a kiss on the cheek and turned to follow the children.

Otto Croenberg stood at attention. "Gentlemen… with my very life I shall guard your children. To get to them, someone will have to pass through me…"

"I know Otto, thank you," John said, smiling.

Paul smiled. "Heck of a note, isn't it?

"A Nazi and a Jew working together?" Otto said, laughingly.

Paul shook his head. "Naw, a Nazi and a Jew working as brothers." He extended his hand and Croenberg gave it one crushing shake.

Michael finally said, "Otto… take care of my mother also, please." Croenberg looked deep into Michael's eyes, gave a quick nod and turned to follow Sarah.

The vehicles were moved back away from the blast area and the VTOL's engines roared to life lifting the plane into the morning sky just as the sun killed the clouds and shone brightly.

Chapter Thirty-Four

"Natalia," Annie said. "I don't know about you but I need a break."

"A break?"

"Yes, would you come along with me? I need some space and I need some place with not quite so many people."

Natalia turned to Annie. "Are you okay?"

Annie smiled but a lone tear ran down her cheek. "I need some sister time and I don't have a sister; would you like to volunteer for the position?"

Natalia smiled and held out her hand. "I've got an idea, why don't we steal an AATV and break out of this compound?"

Annie nodded. "Let's do it. Let's break out and have no plan, no schedule and we won't even be sure we will come back. Let's do it."

They strolled over to the garage, looked until they found the board with ignition keys hanging from it, grabbed a set, found the right AATV and jumped into it. Natalia cranked the vehicle and drove out of the garage.

A soldier in uniform held up his hand to stop the two. Natalia laughed, threw him a kiss and hit the gas throwing gravel in all directions.

*****

Thirty minutes later, the two women sat quietly in the AATV watching the Little Sac River roll silently past. "I don't know, Natalia. I just don't know anymore. I've thought I had things figured out a couple of times."

"Figured out?"

"Yes, I always knew I loved Paul, even when I first met him when I was just a kid. I knew there was no way I could ever have him; not with the age difference. He was grown and I was just a little kid. The world ended and I woke up before the rest of you and had time to grow up before Paul woke up."

Natalia smiled and reached for her hand. "It was quite a surprise for all of us to see you and Michael all grown up."

"Mother was so mad, she never forgave Dad."

"I know but I think she forgave him, she just couldn't forget all of the time she lost with you and Michael."

"Yeah, you're more accurate than I was. Frankly, after that, I always thought you and Dad would end up together. You two sure acted like you were in love."

Natalia was silent for a long moment. "I loved... I love your father, Annie. And I know that he loves me... but somewhere inside of me I always felt like it would never be the two of us forever. Then, Michael had grown up and..."

"He is a lot like Dad..." Annie said.

Natalia frowned. "I did not fall in love with Michael because he reminded me of your father. I fell in love with Michael because of who he is."

"I know that Natalia, sometimes it just seems so... so complicated."

Natalia smiled. "I know. It was complicated for a long time I guess. Michael found and married Madison and she got pregnant and then she died and he hurt so badly. Then the world shifted two or three more times. Sarah found Wolfgang and somewhere along the way I realized that Michael was the Rourke I wanted to spend my life with.

"We all had children and it really seemed like the world had lost all of its craziness. Now... look at us, you and me."

"I know… that's what I'm feeling," Annie said. "We've sent our kids off to keep them safe. Paul and the others have created Retreat 2. Dad was missing and then found. Emma… Emma lost the baby and now she's lost Dad. And Dad, he seems to have lost more than any of us."

Natalia squeezed Annie's hand. "Your father is a very strong man, Honey. A very dedicated, sometimes aggravating and difficult man…" They both laughed.

Annie grew silent after a minute. "Natalia, I am worried about him. I'm worried about Emma and I'm worried about the two of them. I'm worried about us, all of us. I'm not sure what we are going to do in this new world. And, I'm…" She grew quiet.

"And you are scared, right?"

Annie sniffed then drew on some hidden resolve she had forgotten she had. "Yes, I was… I was scared Natalia but I don't think I am anymore. It doesn't make sense."

"Of course it does my dear 'Sister.' Fear makes all of us weak. The unknown keeps us off balance. Aloneness weakens us. But you are not…"

"I am not alone," Annie declared. "I am not alone and I never, ever will be."

Natalia hugged Annie and they laughed and cried. Annie spoke first, "Thanks 'Sis', thanks for being there."

"I will always be there for you, Annie. Just as you have always been there for me."

A voice behind them said, "Ain't that sweet, two ladies huggin' and kissin' and all by themselves."

Natalia whirled and caught a rifle butt across the chin for her effort. The man reversed the rifle and levered a round into the chamber and pointed it at Annie.

"Now, you sit yo'r ass down right there little lady and don't think for one minute I won't put a bullet in that pretty little head of y'uens."

Annie dropped to cradle Natalia's head in her lap. "What did you have to do that for?" she screamed at the man.

"What cha mouth little lady. Watch it real close," he said through gritted teeth and set about tying Annie's hands with a rough rope.

Chapter Thirty-Five

Annie helped the man get Natalia across the saddle of his horse. He took the reins and started walking; over his shoulder he said, "Keep up with me or I'll leave ya, understand?"

"I understand," she said and started following. She tried to remember all of the things she had learned so long ago from her father but hadn't had to use since the children had been born.

"Become a person, an individual, make your captors see you as a person like them," her father had said.

"My name is Annie, Annie Rubenstein…"

"You a Jew girl?"

"My husband is Jewish, his name is Paul. He will be looking for me."

The man laughed. "Well, lil' Jew girl, he ain't gonna find ya. Ain't nobody gonna find you."

Natalia moaned. Annie said, "Please stop, let my friend off the horse, please. She is having trouble breathing."

"Awright," he said and stopped the horse. He reached under the horse's belly and jerked the rope that held Natalia's feet and hands together. He jerked the horse reins and the beast reared up; Natalia slid off the saddle and landed in a heap on the ground.

Natalia shook herself awake and tried to stand. The big man said, "Sit yo'r ass down woman, for'n I knock ya down."

Natalia's eyes flashed around; *Only one man,* she realized. *Look for an advantage and then TAKE IT.*

"Who are you, Sir? What is your name and why have you taken us prisoner?"

"Name's Jedidiah. I took ya prisoner 'cause I wanted to. Gonna take y'uens to my friends at the camp. We don't get to see women much when we're away from home. Y'all kinda purdy, talk too much but y'uens is might purdy.

"I figure me and the boys will enjoy your company for a while… then we'll kill ya and hide the bodies," he said, then started laughing. "Yeah, kill ya and hide the bodies." He grabbed the rope Annie was tied with and flipped a loop around Natalia's hands and arm and tied it quickly.

"Now, git ta walkin' and shut up, I don't want y'uens talkin'."

They walked and walked, Annie thought they had been walking about an hour when she smelled smoke. They broke through the underbrush and she saw the campsite. Six men, in various stages of dress and undress, stood at different chores around the camp.

"Yo… looky what I found," their captor shouted and shoved the girls forward. "Looky what I found!"

Whistles and catcalls greeted the two women as the men came forward, stupid in their lust, grabbing at them. A shot rang out, the men stopped in their tracks and Natalia and Annie turned to see a tall man step out of a large tent on the edge of the campsite. A smoking pistol in his hand.

"What have you done?" he shouted to their captor.

"Found us some women, datswha' I done," the man said indignantly. "More than any of the rest of ya have done."

The tall man walked slowly forward. "What you have found is trouble you idiot." With a twist of his hand, he slammed the large revolver against the man's head and knocked him unconscious.

"Everyone! Everyone back away from the women. Leave them alone and any man that touches one of them will lose the hand he touched them with… at the elbow."

*****

John pointed. "Looks like a campfire over the other side of that hill."

"Sounds like a full blown party," Paul noted.

"Sounds like quite an active party," Michael agreed.

Michael, John Rourke, and Paul climbed and crawled to the top of the hillock and peered over. A quick body count showed there would be plenty of "activity" to go around.

John pointed to a tent on the left side of the clearing. "I'm figuring since Annie and Natalia aren't around the fire, they have them sequestered by themselves. They just about have to be in the tent."

"What do you say, Paul?" Michael asked. "You up to a little stroll in the fine moonlight?"

Paul nodded. "John, we'd appreciate it if you provided a little overwatch while Michael and I go get the girls."

Rourke had already unslung the rifle, flipped the bipod down and was estimating distances. "By the time you two get back down the hill and make your way over to the tent, I'll have my shots laid out."

"Watch for the signal, Dad," Michael said.

"What will it be?"

"Once you see Paul leading the girls out of there and they are clear, I'll start shooting. If anyone spots them, you start shooting."

John dug in his musette bag and laid out several extra magazines for the Steyr-Mannlicher SSG sharp shooting rifle.

"Be careful, be quiet and be careful. When you are ready… take a last look through the NVGs and wave at me. If I wave back, go for it. Now, you two go get our girls."

*****

It took almost thirty minutes before John spotted movement near the tent. He adjusted his position, reached under himself and removed a rock that seemed to have grown out of the ground and straight into his hip bone.

He saw Michael wave, he took one last look around the camp and waved back. He watched as Michael and Paul moved to the back of the tent and Michael slit the tent fabric.

John Rourke shifted to watch the campsite.

Chapter Thirty-Six

Michael listened intently, hearing nothing inside the tent; he stuck his knife in the tent fabric and slowly, quietly cut downward. Paul turned to watch their rear while Michael crawled through the opening.

Natalia was on the far side of the tent, gagged and hogtied but conscious. Her eyes caught Michael's; he winked and held one finger to his lips. She nodded and quickly moved her eyes to the still form of the guard.

He was asleep.

As Michael moved quietly toward the guard, he could see Annie Rubenstein rise up behind Natalia. She was tied and blood trickled from a cut above her left eye.

Bastards, Michael thought. *If they have touched either of them…* Slowly, Michael reached for the sleeping guard's neck. With a distance of just inches left, Michael slammed his open hand in the guard's throat and with a steel grip closed it around his larynx.

Paul watched from the slit. As soon as Michael had the guard subdued, he crawled to the girls and cut their bindings. He held Annie tightly then pushed her back to examine the cut on her forehead. She smiled.

Natalia moved to Michael's side and secured the guard while Michael kept him incapacitated. Then as Michael laid the unconscious man down, she stood and kicked him in the side of the head.

Then she dropped back to the ground and kissed Michael hard on the lips. Michael gave her the silenced Walther and her Bali-Song. Paul had already given Annie a Beretta 9mm. He waved the girls to the slit in the tent but he went through it first and made sure the coast was clear.

Annie came out next holding Paul's outstretched hand; Natalia followed quickly. Michael was going to be the distraction that would help the others escape. Michael stepped through the doorway of the tent.

That was when a shot rang out and a man sitting by the fire stood straight up and keeled over, dead. All eyes searched the hillcrest looking for a sniper. It gave Michael the advantage he needed. He pulled his single action .44 and thumbed back the hammer.

An instant later, 230 grains of lead and copper-nickel jacket smashed into the side of another man. The fight was on.

Paul and Annie had reached cover and headed down the side of the hill when Paul looked back. Natalia was not to be seen. Paul cursed and jerked Annie's hand and they ran toward John Thomas Rourke's position.

A sixth sense told Michael to turn... he spun with the silver magnum tracking ahead of him. At the last instant, he jerked it skyward.

"Natalia..." he spun back toward the campfire and fired. Natalia was calmly standing and squeezing off rounds as though she was at the shooting range instead of in a shooting war.

"Natalia, will you please be careful?"

Blam, Blam. "Darling, I am being careful and I'm being thorough." Blam, Blam, Blam... a man screamed and flew through the air.

It was the first time in a long time they had fought side by side. *How is it that I could have missed this action alongside her and not known it,* Michael wondered.

A final shot rang out from the Walther and the slide locked open. Without hesitation, Natalia transitioned to the Bali-Song... click, click, click... open... closed... open. A man rushed at her, she smiled and took a deep breath and settled herself. In his hand was a small double bit camp hatchet. Rather than holding it over his head to smash with, he moved it side to side to slash with. She smiled deeper in approval; *A worthy opponent,* she thought.

She faked to the man's right as he swung the ax to his left, it broke his rhythm and he moved quickly to pull the hatchet back for another slice. She stepped inside his reach, turning her back to the man and stepping back to make contact with his chest as she pushed the elbow upward; the hatchet now useless. Click, click, click... open... closed... open... she pushed hard with her right foot moving her hips to her left and stabbed down and back.

The blade of the Bali-Song entered the junction of his crotch and his thigh. She turned and twisted and slashed reducing the femoral artery to a pitiful ribbon of tissue incapable of holding, much less carrying, blood. The man screamed, lost the hatchet and collapsed all in one motion... and died before his heart had pumped twenty more times.

She stepped away, her heart pumping. *How... how I have missed this,* she thought. She spun around; no more attackers to be seen. She walked to Michael and kissed him hard... very hard on the lips. "Now," she said. "Now, take me home and love me."

Michael smiled and did exactly that.

Chapter Thirty-Seven

Michael asked, "From the description that Mayor White gave us, do you think you can estimate the location of the cave system where they found the weapons?"

Chief Warrant Officer Wes Sanderson smiled. "Way ahead of you, Sir. I started working on it as soon as I saw the armaments in the Underground. While I can't be one hundred percent sure, I'm pretty confident that I can get us to within a hundred yards.

"I've been matching old maps to the current layouts of all of the rivers, streams, and creeks along the boundary of the old Fort Leonard Wood complex."

Paul broke in, "But with all of the geological changes..."

"But some things don't usually change very much unless there are some tectonic plate shifts or fault separations like with Florida and California," Sanderson clarified. "Most times, caverns collapse, earth slides bury features, rivers shift the paths but... water always flows downhill and along the paths of least resistance."

"So, you're saying it should be pretty much the way it was when we were searching for the caverns here at Retreat 2?"

Sanderson nodded. "Exactly, everything looks different but once you find a couple of specific landmark features... location of a particular place is a lot easier."

"But they didn't tell us exactly where the cave system was," Paul reminded.

"No, but the reality is there are only a couple of places where it might be. First of all, they mentioned a cliff face and a river that existed back at the time of the Night of the War. We have found three such locations.

One of those is probably too far from what remains of the old highway system that was close to the caves."

Sanderson pointed to a large area map with three indicated positions. "Munitions have a lot of weight; not likely they manhandled a lot of that stuff into the cave. I think it is safe to scratch this one off the list. That leaves these two. This one," he indicated on the map, "I think is the most probable."

"Why are you so sure?" Paul asked.

"It is still within the old boundaries of the Fort Wood. I can't see the staff secreting munitions on civilian property under any circumstances. With what they considered a state of war, there is even less likelihood they would.

"Additionally, there is evidence of reoccurring activity along access points. Could be personnel making frequent visits in the area."

Ryan Fleming, the titular head of the POTUS Posse asked, "So, Mr. President, when would you like to pop over there and take a peek?"

Michael Rourke studied the map. "How close do you think we can get with AATVs?"

Sanderson studied the topographic overlays. "You should be able to drive to within a half mile, maybe even closer."

Michael nodded. "Ryan, why don't you get a team together, arm up the AATVs and leave in... an hour?"

Ryan stood up and adjusted his combat harness. "Would prefer it if you rode with me, Sir."

Michael nodded. "Appreciate the offer Ryan but for this operation I have another co-pilot in mind. No offense; one hour to roll out then."

Fleming saluted and acknowledged. "No offense taken, Sir," and left.

"Paul, I'd prefer it if you stayed here and monitored our progress. Probably wouldn't hurt to have a Quick Reaction Team on standby in case we run into more than we think we will."

"I agree, Michael," Paul said.

*****

The ride from Retreat 2 to the Fort Leonard Wood perimeter took a little over three hours. Before the Night of the War it would have taken less than two.

Michael Rourke and Natalia rode in the first AATV. Fleming and Steve Vaughn were swinging wide to the right flank. Jim Judy, Mike Spivey, and Neal James rode the left flank. Judy and Spivey drove the third AATV with James as an out rider on his Harley.

"It has been a while since you and I have been in action together, Natalia," Michael said as he glanced at her; she was still the most beautiful woman he had ever seen. Her features softened only a little by childbirth and a few years.

Dressed in her black skin tight combat rig and knee-high boots, she looked as gorgeous as ever. Her hair was long and tied into a simple ponytail. She laughed. "Well, dear husband… let's see if we still have it; what do you say?"

Michael laughed and stomped the accelerator, the AATV charged up the hill going airborne at the top and landing smoothly. It felt good to be alive. It felt good to be armed and flying into danger with her by his side. "It has been too long, Darling."

She flashed him an intense and alluring smile. "I love you, Michael Rourke."

He downshifted, slid into a turn and accelerated out, upshifted and said, "I love you, Natalia Rourke. I love you with all my heart."

There was an explosion off to their left.

Chapter Thirty-Eight

Jim Judy was driving, his vision focused on the terrain while Michael Spivey watched the area for signs of an ambush. They were moving quickly through the forest, occasionally reaching speeds of twenty miles per hour in the open areas and glens.

Spivey spotted something in his peripheral vision and turned.

The explosion ripped the left front tire and wheel off the AATV, lifting the entire vehicle and heaving it up and over to the right. It landed on the roll bar cage and continued rolling for another forty feet before slamming into a tree.

As the dust and debris settled and the air started to clear, silence settled across the vacant section of ground; the only sound was the whirling of the right front tire and a steady drip, drip of fuel.

Spivey came to. "Land mine…" he whispered to Judy but Judy was unconscious and couldn't hear him. Slowly Spivey found the microphone and spoke two words, "Mine field." He had warned the others… if the radio still worked and the transmission had gotten out.

If not, they would come quickly toward the sound of the explosion and die along with him. The mic fell from his lifeless fingers as he joined Jim Judy in the warm grasp of unconsciousness.

Chapter Thirty-Nine

Neal James slid to a stop as he heard Spivey's voice weakly over his ear piece. He barely made out, "Mine field." He keyed his throat mic, "Short Stop to Babe Ruth, over."

"Go ahead, Short Stop, over."

"Did you copy Second Base's message? Over."

"Roger that, copy Mike Foxtrot. Over."

"Roger that, Mike Foxtrot. I'm swinging around to come up in their tracks. Suggest all units stand by. Over."

"Roger that, Short Stop. Use caution. Over."

Neal James was already gunning his motorcycle, the rear tire ripping dirt and grass as the heavy bike spun around and changed directions. Within minutes, James had found the tracks of the AATV and was riding in the right one.

He stopped when he saw the blast crater still smoking ahead and flipping the kick stand down, he dismounted. To his right, he saw the overturned AATV; Jim Judy and Spivey hanging upside down in their harnesses… unmoving.

James scanned the area; it looked like the grass in this little glen had green measles. There were splotches of round growth patterns scattered in a hopscotch pattern. James recognized the pattern.

Often, the materials in conventional land mines act almost like fertilizer and enhance the growth of grasses directly above the mine. It is not impossible to spot, but you had to know what you were looking for in order to recognize the threat.

He walked back to the bike and stood with one foot on the seat and the other balanced on a foot peg. This got him the altitude he needed to observe the pattern in more detail. Once he had it confirmed in his own mind, he ran for the overturned AATV.

Glancing quickly around the vehicle, he could see at least two places where the weight of the AATV appeared to be sitting on mines. Since they had not gone off he assumed they were some sort of the "Bouncing Betty" version. When the trigger was depressed, the mine would arm. When the trigger was released a propellant charge would launch the mine into the air where it would explode. Usually at a height that corresponded either with an average man's chest… or his testicles.

The question was could he cut the two men free without triggering the propellant charges which would probably kill all three of them.

Searching his memory for details on the AATVs, he could not remember the weight of the vehicle but decided it should be enough to keep the trigger plunger depressed even when Judy and Spivey were cut loose.

He did a quick but thorough examination of the two men. Spivey appeared to be the lesser injured. Judy had shrapnel wounds in several places and blood running from his ears. As the driver, he had been closest to the explosion.

Pulling his combat knife, he sliced Spivey's seat belt first and guided his lower body down, slicing the chest strap at the last moment.

James smiled. "No boom is a good thing!" He picked Spivey up and carefully carried the man back to where his Harley stood. Carefully stepping in his own footprints, he was able to lay Spivey down just as the man regained consciousness.

"Mike, stay here… don't move."

"Mine field. Be careful," Spivey said.

"Rest here, I'm going after Jim." At a quick step James retraced his footprints yet again. In his initial examination, James had realized that Judy was the most seriously injured. He had determined that if he could get Spivey to safe ground, he could have more time to work on Judy.

On a closer examination of Jim Judy, he was glad he had made that decision.

"How are you doing, Neal?" Judy's voice surprised Neal James as he was examining the man's injuries.

"Better than you are Jim." James smiled at his old friend.

"Yeah, I know... I'm screwed up pretty badly."

"Naw, I'll get you down and to safe ground and the docs will get you patched up like nothing ever happened."

Judy smiled a crooked grin. "You are a lousy liar, Neal James... or you're dumber than even I give you credit for being. You can't fix what's wrong with me. I'm pretty sure I broke my back in that rollo-ver... Neal, I can't feel or move my legs."

James could testify to the accuracy of Jim Judy's self-diagnosis as he pulled a seven inch long and two-inch wide splinter of metal from Judy's left thigh. Judy never felt it as James quickly put a pressure bandage on the leg.

Even if he was able to extract Judy and somehow move him over forty feet through an active mine field, he would most likely be a paraplegic for the rest of his life.

Judy gave a weary smile. "Neal, I'm not going to be much help to you I'm afraid. Depending on where and how bad the break is... when you cut me down... it might kill me. If it doesn't, you can't pick me up and carry me, you'll have to drag me to safety."

"Yeah, I know. You have any suggestions?"

"Yeah, let's figure I won't make it back..."

"Don't go giving up..."

"I'm not, but let's be practical. If I were at Mid-Wake on the operat-ing table instead of halfway around the world hanging upside down in this wreck... well, I'd probably have a chance. I'm not and I don't... the best case scenario is I survive and become a burden to the Posse and my wife and daughters.

"I'm going to get Spivey and bring him back over here. He's conscious and can give me a hand." James was up and running, carefully staying in his footprints. After all, the growth pattern of grass might not be totally accurate.

"Mike, we have to get Jim down and I need your help. His back is hurt and he can't feel his legs. I need your help to drag him back here to safety."

"Let's go," Spivey said and shakily tried to stand. The snap of a rifle shot and the slug it spit arrived at almost the same time. The slug hit the frame of the AATV and ricocheted off toward where Spivey and James crouched next to the motorcycle.

More shots were directed at Spivey and James and they hit the ground as flat as they could. They were caught in the open without cover.

Chapter Forty

The other AATVs were converging on the wreck, gunfire signaling the location. Michael keyed his mic, "Short Stop, this is Second Base, SITREP, over."

"Second Base, we are taking rifle fire from the tree line. I have Spivey but Judy is still hanging in his harness upside down. He believes his back is broken and he can't use his legs. Over."

"Roger, headed to your location. Out. Natalia, get on the machine gun and get ready to lay down suppressive fire," Michael ordered. "Keying his mic, "Second Base to Umpire, SITREP, over."

Ryan Fleming and Steve Vaughn were busy also... Fleming keyed his mic, "Approaching from the left and topping the hill... now." The AATV rocketed over the crest of the small hill and Vaughn was firing the machine gun before the AATV landed.

"STOP! Ryan, stop where you are... mine field!" Neal James radioed.

Ryan's AATV slowed and stopped; Vaughn continued to lay down fire on the tree line. Ryan dismounted and stood on the bumper of the AATV, with his six-foot nine-inch frame and the twenty-inch bumper, he was tall enough to get a good view of the land below them.

He stood oblivious to the rifle fire and planned his next move. Keying his mic, "Short Stop, Umpire here, over."

"Go Umpire, over."

"How long before you can have Judy out of that wreck? Over."

"Negative Umpire, we can't even approach the AATV, we are taking direct and accurate fire. If we move, we're dead. Over."

"Short Stop, SITREP on Jim Judy's condition. Over?"

"Umpire, he is still alive... they're not firing at him. They are using him as bait for us. Over."

"Umpire to Second Base, over."

"Go Umpire, over."

"Where are you, Sir? Over."

"Umpire, we came in on their right rear flank. Approaching on foot; will engage in a minute or two. Can you lay down fire from your location? Over."

"Second Base, not effectively. We can keep them engaged from this angle but that is about it. Over."

"Roger, Short Stop… get ready to retrieve Judy as soon as we engage, copy? Over."

"Standby Sir," Jim Judy's voice came over the radio net. "Everyone standby… Be ready to engage when I give the signal. Over."

"What signal?" James screamed into the radio. An instant later he had his answer as Jim Judy fired the machine gun on the AATV.

"Mr. President," Judy said over the roar of the machine gun. "It was an honor to serve with you. Now, fellas… do it now."

Ryan drove his AATV through a zigzag course he had memorized as Vaughn opened up with his machine gun.

Michael Rourke rose up behind a log. He laid the barrel of the machine gun he had removed from his AATV on the log and squeezed off controlled three round bursts at the line of attackers firing on Jim Judy's position.

Natalia fired into the attackers with her Car 15 and four men were hit immediately. Suddenly the Car 15 was snatched from her hands by a round that smacked into the receiver.

She drew her Walther from the shoulder holster and fired. A 115 grain 9mm slug tore through the man's left shoulder and he dropped the bolt action rifle he was using, then he stood up.

Skinny to the point of malnutrition, he wore a filthy undershirt and disgustingly dirty jeans and in his uninjured right hand he now carried a long-handled, hooked-bladed, brush knife.

He approached Natalia slowly, his left arm dangling uselessly by his side. The big bull knife swung from side to side. The wicked hook could take Natalia's arm off at the shoulder with one swing, or her head from her neck.

Hearing movement behind, Natalia turned quickly and fired at two others that were moving on her. They dropped dead in their tracks but the slide on the Walther locked open... that magazine was empty.

Without hesitation she pulled the Bali-Song from the slit pocket on the leg of her body suit. A rhythmic, click, click, click began.

Click, click, click, she moved toward the man's injured left arm drawing him in closer. Click, click, click then there was a SWOOSH as the hawk-billed, bull knife was swung; the man had to pivot in order to control the big knife.

He swung the knife and followed through to complete the circle attack with two quick steps. Natalia continued to move toward the outside of his injured arm. Click, click, click...SWOOSH... SWOOSH.

The man smiled and spoke, "I'm a gonna get you, pretty lady. I'm gonna get you with this blade." SWOOSH.

Natalia smiled. "Come on, you Ublyudok."

"Wha did ya call me?"

Natalia was swaying in time with the man, timing his next move. "I called you a bastard, you bastard."

The man's eyes flashed and the hawk-billed knife rose straight up then turned and went in a circle aiming for Natalia's neck. "You bitch."

She sidestepped and ducked; the heavy blade sliced through the air above her head. She flashed her right hand up and the Bali-Song's point slid smoothly into the man's armpit ripping through muscle and the main artery.

The big brush knife flew from his hand. "Ouch, you bitch… you stuck me," the man said as he stumbled, blood spurting from the cut.

"No, you Ublyudok, I killed you. I cut your brachial artery. You are bleeding to death."

The man raised his arm to look at the wound and blood spurt several feet from the cut with each beat of his heart—his heart was racing with the strain of battle. He stumbled again, took two steps forward and dropped to his knees. "You bitch," he said and fell forward.

Click, click, click and the Bali-Song closed; Natalia slid it back into the slit pocket on her leg. "Ublyudok," she said and spit on the man as she passed him.

*****

"Sir," Jim Judy's voice sounded strange… weaker than before.

Michael Rourke keyed his mic. "Go ahead Jim, over."

"I've got about three-quarters of a belt left in place in the machine gun. I can't load another belt of ammo. Once it's gone, there's not much I can do to help you. Over."

"Just standby, Jim. We're coming for you…"

"NO! No Sir, you can't do that. Besides if you were absolutely successful and no one else got killed or hurt… I know what would be in store for me. Thanks but no thanks. Over."

Michael took a deep breath and let it out slowly, "Alright, Jim. Do you have a plan? Over."

"Yeah… yes, Sir, I do—make a point of pulling the AATVs out of here. Put Spivey and Ryan Fleming on their sniper rifles from camouflaged positions. When the bad guys come for me, we take 'em out. There can't be too many of them left. Wha cha think? Over."

Spivey told Neal James, "The way Judy is slurring his words, he won't be conscious very much longer. Whatever we're going to do, we better do it now. Let's try it Judy's way."

James keyed his mic. "POTUS, James here. Spivey recommends we initiate Jim Judy's plan and says we need to make it quick if it has a chance to be successful."

"Roger, does Spivey have his sniper rifle?"

"Negative, it is in the AATV with Judy. I'll leave him my long gun. Let me pull out first on the bike and I'll circle around to the east and come in from their left flank. We can catch them in a crossfire."

Michael looked down at the ground and took a deep breath. "Do it, Neal. Jim, can you read me?"

"Yes, Sir, I'm still here and I ain't goin'nowhere."

"We'll do it your way. Good luck Jim and… and thanks for everything you have done."

"Sir, would you be the one to talk to the wife and the girls? It would mean a lot to them."

"Will do… Go with God, Jim."

Chapter Forty-One

Neal James double timed to the Harley and mounted. He hit the ignition and was gone in a flurry of dirt and grass. A few shots rang out but they were ineffective.

"Give me a couple of minutes to get in position, Sir. Hey, Jim Judy... you be careful firing the machine gun. You've never been a great shot, you know."

Judy keyed the mic, he coughed into it. "Best hope I'm good enough to miss your ugly butt, Spivey. Hey Mike..."

"Yeah, Jim," Spivey said with a catch in his voice. "Yeah... me too."

Vaughn and Natalia mounted the AATVs and roared back over the hillside. In moments the scene was still. Ryan Fleming watched silently before keying his mic... "Here they come, watch yourself, Brother Judy."

"I'm ready, not a lot of ammo left in this belt... but I'll give 'em all I've got."

Seven men walked slowly toward the upside down AATV where Jim Judy hung helpless and still as death. "I'm on target," Ryan said. "Neal, you ready?"

James pulled his automatic 12-gauge around to hang from its sling on his left side. The short barrel and pistol grip make it a devastating blaster. "I am."

"So am I." Spivey said, quietly, "Jim Judy..."

"Yeah, Mike."

"This is your dance, start the music when you are ready," Spivey said.

Spivey smiled when he heard Judy's transmission. "Here we go, Ladies and Gentlemen... anna one anna two anna..." the machine gun opened up.

Fleming fired three times, heavy grained .30 slugs tore through chest cavities and brain cases. The first two men he killed never realized they were hit. A slug passed through the first man's chest destroying his heart, slamming into the next man's right temple. The lay of the land created the perfect shot.

Spivey sighted the CAR 15 and sent a .556mm slug whistling toward first one man then another. Neal James' Harley topped the hill and was airborne. When he landed he grabbed at the pistol grip of the shotgun and blasted away.

Through it all, controlled bursts from Jim Judy's machine kept the tempo of the fight lively. Michael Rourke ran forward toward Spivey and Judy, firing his single action .44 Magnum, killing one bad guy and wounding another. Spivey held his fire as Rourke slid the last few feet toward the AATV.

Rifle fire was pinging off the AATV frame and biting into the dirt around it. Judy's body jumped first one way then the next. Michael rose up and fired two quick shots at the man who had shot Judy. A 230 grain slug caught the man just below the junction of his shoulders and neck.

An explosion of bone and tissue exited the man's back as he somersaulted backwards. He lay still.

Spivey was up and running for the AATV. When he got there Michael was cradling Jim Judy's head in his hands. There was a hint of a smile on Judy's face.

Chapter Forty-Two

It took a while to right the damaged AATV; the mines failed to blow. They would have to return to salvage it. Jim Judy's body was placed in a body bag and secured to one of the other vehicles. He would be returned to Retreat 2 for a hero's burial and the questionable honor of the first burial in the Retreat 2 cemetery. Rubenstein feared there would be more.

It took another two hours before the POTUS Posse found and rushed into the cave system and established a secure position.

A quick survey revealed the cave system floor was covered in scuff marks and footprints. Men had obviously been removing something, and the consensus was that "something" had been munitions.

There was a foul smell that emanated from the depths of the cave system. It was a putrid combination of dampness, decomposition, and a strong musk-like odor.

Fleming established a security team to watch over the AATVs and cover the cave entrance while the remaining explored.

The team had been moving slowly and deliberately for almost forty-five minutes and were rounding a bend deep within the cave when Fleming threw his left hand up with the fist closed; the sign for STOP.

The stink was strongest here and in the distance, just beyond the range of the head lamp he wore, he could just make out the shape of something huge walking on all fours.

In a whisper, Spivey asked, "What is it?"

Ryan Fleming whispered back, "Looks something like a grizzly bear, but it has a misshapen head and it is huge. Far larger than any bear should be, almost twice as big."

"Could it be a bear whose ancestors survived The Night of the War and passed on some genetic mutations from radiation?"

"Probably… as good an explanation as any."

"So what do we do?"

"Everyone stand still, be absolutely still." Fleming laughed under his breath.

"What's up, Ryan?"

In a whisper, Fleming said, "I'm having me a flashback. "So my bird…"

"Your girlfriend?

"Yeah, my bird, she went totally mental a while back. All I did was call her a big fat rhino. She went fucking ballistic, proper going into one, screaming and shouting at me, calling me every prick under the sun and threatening to knock the granny out of me."

"What did you do?"

"I tell you, mate, I just stood there, didn't move a muscle. Well, it's the safest thing to do, as her vision's based mainly on movement. And I suspect the same is true with this monster."

Suddenly the bear stopped and stood on its hind feet, its nose sniffing a scent it did not recognize.

"Uh oh," Fleming said. "Everyone start backing out as quickly and as quietly as you can manage."

The bear began moving toward the men, sniffing and growling… the sounds reverberated off the cave walls creating even more confusion.

"Bloody hell, it's a cave bear or its blinkin' cousin!" Fleming shouted.

"What the hell is a cave bear?" one of Sanderson's troopers hollered. Everyone charged their weapons and stood stock still.

Sanderson said, "Ursus spelaeus, a species of bear that lived in Europe and Asia until about 24,000 years ago when they went extinct; right concept but the wrong bear. Cave bears had a very broad, domed skull with a steep forehead. It was similar in structure and size to the modern brown bear. They would average 350 to over 1300 pounds."

The trooper was confused. "But you said it was the wrong bear…"

"Yep, wrong bear. This one is significantly larger, closer to 1800 pounds. I think it is a pizzly bear or a nanulak," Sanderson said almost in a whisper.

"What the hell is that?" Another trooper demanded.

Sanderson gave the hand signal and the men began backing out of the cave. Sanderson said, "A grizzly and a polar bear mated, probably three to four generations ago when the ice cap still extended this far south. A think residual radiation somewhere over the generations mutated one of its ancestors to this larger size and those modified genes just kept being passed down.

The bear roared so loud that it vibrated the dark spots in Ryan's eyes, "Holy… here it comes… get outta here!"

*****

Ryan J. Fleming stood up to his full six foot nine inches. The bear focused on him but slowed its advance. This human was not running from him, but was walking toward him.

The Lancer Model M1A1 .308 rifle had a round in the chamber, and Fleming's piercing blue eyes had the bear dead in his sights, but did not fire… yet. The bear had stopped its rush and stood up on its hind legs, establishing its dominance. The bear roared again. Fleming stood stock still, counting the seconds until the last of the team was out of the cave. He lowered the weapon, filled his lungs and… roared back at the bear.

*****

The rest of the POTUS Posse and Sanderson's Marines were out of the cave and set up in a curved firing line to prevent friendly fire accidents when Fleming came running out the cave with the bear in hot pursuit. Fleming would pass and they would open up on the bear. It would be simply butchery. But Fleming was no where in sight. Five minutes passed, then ten… then twenty and there still was no sight of Fleming or the bear… but there had not been any gun fire from inside the cave either. Sanderson finally hand signaled six of his troopers to separate from the others.

"I want you to swap weapons with some of the others. I want two Squad Automatic Weapons. I want one grenade launcher with both HE and buckshot loads. Everyone else is to have a shotgun… hurry up… we're going hunting."

"Hello outside the cave… Hello outside the cave… hold your fire. I'm coming out, don't shoot." Ryan Fleming peeked around the edge of the cavern entrance and waved.

Sanderson kept his people focused on the cave as Fleming came out whistling. Sanderson recognized the tune. In military circles it is known as the "Colonel Bogey March." To old movie buffs it is known as the theme from The Bridge on the River Kwai. As luck would have it The Bridge on the River Kwai is one of the few classics that survived from before The Night of the War.

"The bear is not a threat fellas, the old girl was just protecting her cubs. They left through another exit." Fleming slung the M1A1 over one shoulder and smiled.

Sanderson came up to the towering Brit. "Y'all had a nice talk and decided no one needed to be eaten or shot today, is that about it?"

Fleming winked slyly and grinned. "That's about it, Chief. That was about it."

Chapter Forty-Three

John Rourke rolled the big Harley out of the cavern just as Paul Rubenstein came by. "Going for a ride?" Rubenstein asked.

Rourke looked up and smiled, "Yeah, taking off for a couple of days... maybe a week. I need some road time, Paul. I feel... I'm not real sure what I feel right now so I'm going to go see if I can find myself."

Paul frowned. "If you can wait a couple of days, I could go with you."

John shook his head. "You've got too much to do here, so does Michael. I'm just an extra body right now. I left a map with the Communication Center of where I'm heading. I'll check in from time to time."

Rourke looked at the ground for a moment before raising his head and locking eyes with Paul. "Most often... when everything is said and done, more often things are said but not done. But you Paul, once you joined me on a quest to find my family and to save what we could of the world..."

Paul smiled wanly. "I really didn't have too much choice."

Rourke shook his head. "You had as much as anybody else did those first hours. You became my brother and... we even won and survived. But right now, after all of these years, sometimes I feel we have accomplished nothing. Now both of our families are in jeopardy and the world is teetering on the precipice of another fine disaster that could end it all for all time. Old friend, I must find me now. But, I will be back."

With that, he cranked the Harley and swung his leg over the saddle. He pulled his aviator sunglasses from his pocket and saluted; pulling away from the main entrance to the Retreat 2... he gunned the bike and moments later was out of sight.

*****

He rode southwest for several hours. After the second hour the weather was noticeably warmer and signs of civilization became more common.

A little north of Little Rock, Arkansas, he stopped for gas and to stretch his back. "Whew," he said to himself. "It's been a while since I rode this far on two wheels."

He filled his tank and replaced the hose. Walking across the drive, he pulled one of his thin dark cigars from his shirt pocket and the battered Zippo from the watch pocket in his jeans. He turned back toward the horizon; the view in this part of the Ozarks was gorgeous.

He rolled the striker wheel and when the yellow blue flame caught, he puffed the cigar until he had it going to his satisfaction. Standing there, he realized that during one of the trips he and Paul had made looking for Sarah and the kids, he had come this way.

A thousand years ago, he thought with a degree of melancholy. *All of that and what do I have to show for it; an ex-wife that loves me but can't live with me, a current wife that no longer knows me and can't forgive herself for the death of her child, and the only other woman I have ever loved is married to my son. Hell of a fine mess you have Mr. Rourke.*

He stood there smoking and thinking and looking at the mountain vista across the valley and back at all of the years across time. *Yep, hell of a mess…*

He paid for the gas and continued driving south and west. Just outside of what had been Fort Smith, he stopped for the night and began to set up camp.

After building a fire ring out of fist-sized rocks and setting up his small tent, he dug into his saddlebags and got the bottle of Seagram's out. He boiled some water and dropped in freeze-dried beef stroganoff.

Leaning against the base of a tree, he finished supper and fished out another cigar. He cut the seal on the Seagram's and poured two fingers in his canteen cup. With camp set up, a full stomach, and good whiskey in hand, he puffed the cigar to life.

A stout pull on the whiskey warmed his guts and the smoke set his mood. *How many times like this, how many nights like this did I spend trying to save the world?*

Finally, the whiskey and the cigar were finished and the exertion of the day told him it was time for sleep. He secured the Harley, climbed in his tent, and laid his boots by his feet. He shed the double Alessi shoulder rig with the CombatMasters and laid the Python and a flashlight next to his head.

Using his bomber jacket as a pillow and a lightweight thermal blanket to cover with, John Thomas Rourke slept.

He slept like he hadn't in a long time.

Chapter Forty-Four

I edged left, my eyes watching Karamatsov's eyes, the fog starting to lift and swirl as the wind picked up, sunlight breaking through. I squint, despite the glasses, against the glare of the sun on the gray fog.

It was misleading, I thought, *to say you should watch the eyes. Karamatsov had probably assumed as much. At twenty-five yards or so, the eyes themselves would be hard or impossible to see, clearly. Instead, you watched the set of the eyes,* he thought, *the almost imperceptible tightening of the muscles around them, the little squint that—*

I see his eyes set.

Karamatsov's right hand flashed up toward the Model 59 in the shoulder rig, the thumb snap breaking with an almost audible click, the gun's muzzle straightening out as Karamatsov took a half-step right and crouched, his left hand moving to help grasp the gun; the hat caught up by a gust of wind and sailing from his head.

My right hand moves first, then my left, the right hand bringing the first Detonics on line; the safety swept off under my thumb as the gun cleared the leather, the gun in the left hand moving on line as I trigger the first shot.

I see the flash against the fog of Karamatsov's pistol, the stainless Detonics bucking through recoil in my right hand, then the left gun firing, then the right and the left simultaneously.

Karamatsov flew up off the ground almost a foot, I judge, the gun in Karamatsov's hands firing up into the air—a second round. The Russian's body twitches in midair, then lurches twice more as it falls, the Russian's gun firing again into the street. A window smashes on the other side. His body rolls over face down, the right arm and left leg twitching, shivering, and then stopping.

There was no more movement.

I thumb up the safety on the pistol in my right hand and jab it into my belt, shifting the gun in my left hand to my right, thumb up the safety and hold the gun limp at my side against my thigh and walk forward, slowly, then stop, rolling over the Russian's body with my combat-booted foot, my right thumb poised over the safety of the pistol.

There are four dark-red patches on Karamatsov's trunk.

I bend over and, with the thumb of my left hand, close the eyelids.

"Done," I whisper.

*****

What? Noise... Rourke came awake with a start, the Python in his hand. The sky was not even starting to show light, he listened. He checked his Submariner watch, midnight. "A dream... nothing but a damn dream," he murmured.

Finding his boots he pulled them on and unzipped the tent. He had heard something; he knew THAT part was not part of the dream.

Crawling out with the Alessi holster system in his left hand and the Python in his right, he stood up, listening.

What is that noise, he wondered. He slipped into the double Alessi rig and shrugged allowing his CombatMasters to settle across his shoulders. He threaded the Python's holster on his belt and settled it in the small of his back.

He pulled the bomber jacket from the tent and slipped it on, there was just the hint of a chill. He slid the A.G. Russell black chrome Sting 1A behind his hip on the left side and the green handled Survivalist Sting in the top of his left boot and started walking toward the sound.

He had walked about 150 yards when he stopped to listen again, it was clearer now. Voices, loud angry voices...

He dropped low before topping the crest of a hill and moved laterally until he could see what was happening. There was a campfire, he could see four… no, five men and one woman. The woman was crying.

The men looked like locals, work clothes and an old pickup… they were arguing but Rourke was not close enough to hear about what. But he had an idea… the woman.

He stood up and started moving toward the group. Two of the men went back and picked the woman up, one on each arm and walked her toward the pickup.

"Come on Jessy… ya said ya would."

"I didn't say I'd do all of ya, just you Jacob. I thought you loved me."

"I do, Jessy. I do love you."

"I love ya too, Jessy," the largest man said.

"Me too, Jessy," another said and laughed.

The oldest stood up and dropped out of the bed of the truck. "Lay her up here boys, Bert and me gonna have a go at her and the rest of you can have what's left."

The big guy picked Jessy up and put her in the truck bed, the two men that were in there grabbed her and held her down. She started crying again. The oldest man started to unzip his pants while the one called Bert jerked the girl's skirt and panties off.

Rourke shook his head, *Damnit. I just wanted a good night's sleep and some peace and quiet.* He unzipped the bomber jacket and let it hang open. Reaching behind him he unsnapped the thumb break on the Python's holster.

Taking a deep breath, Rourke let it out slowly and said, "Hello, Gentlemen."

116

Everything stopped including the girl's whimpering sobs. The oldest zipped his jeans back up and looked toward the sound. "Who is that? Who's out there?"

Chapter Forty-Five

"A fella trying to get some sleep," Rourke said and moved closer toward the group. "How about you guys leave the little lady alone and call it a night." Closer now, Rourke could see the empty beer cans and the smell of spilled whiskey around the campfire.

The oldest said, "How about you shut up and get outta here and mind your own business." The one called Bert reached in the truck bed and pulled out a hickory ax handle. The one the girl called Jacob pulled a stag handled knife from his belt.

Rourke could see this was not going to end well. "Fellas, look! There's been no harm done. You guys were nice enough to want to share some time with Jessy but Jessy has changed her mind and doesn't want to share any more time with y'all. Let's just call it a night and everyone part friends."

Rourke was close enough now that he could see the oldest guy had a revolver stuck in his belt. Bert started waving the ax handle and shouting, "How 'bout I'll part your hair you SOB! I'll part yo…"

The guy with the gun pulled it; Rourke pulled the Python and fired once.

"Son of a…" the man with the revolver watched as his revolver and one of his fingers flew off into the night. "He shot me! You shot me!" he shouted incredulously.

Rourke kept the Python out, covering the group. "Guys, like I said. Let's call it a night before someone really gets hurt. Y'all go home, get him to the doctor and have that hand looked at. Let's all live to see the sun come up. What do you say?"

One of the men in the pickup bed jumped out and reached in through the cab window. Rourke shook his head and shifted his aim. As the double barrel shotgun swung on line to shoot him, Rourke fired, hitting the man in the face with 158 grains of lead and copper-nickel jacket.

As his face collapsed in on itself, both barrels of the shotgun fired at the same time. Rourke was already airborne, out of the way of the blast. He rolled once and fired again at Bert who was running toward Rourke swinging the ax handle.

Had Bert not been swinging the ax handle the shot would have missed, but Bert swung the ax handle and his elbow intercepted the path of the slug and part of the radius bone, the smaller of the two bones between the elbow and the wrist; it shattered and a half-inch section blew out of his arm.

Rourke's right hand jerked the Detonics CombatMaster from the left side of the Alessi shoulder holster. Rourke thumbed the safety off and shouted, "Enough!"

But it wasn't… Jacob and the other guy in the pickup bed were moving. Jacob had jerked Jessy out of the truck bed by her feet and stood behind her using her as a shield while holding his knife to her throat.

The other guy had retrieved and reloaded the double barrel; Rourke fired twice with the Detonics, both slugs hitting the man's heart and turning it into sausage. Rourke swapped guns, the Python ending up in his right hand.

Rourke's voice was soft and low as he spoke, "Now Jacob, it is Jacob isn't it?" Jacob nodded. "I thought so. Well Jacob, here we are… there's two wounded; two men dead and just you and me still standing. Sound about right to you? Look at Bert, Jacob… he's bleeding pretty bad, maybe dying."

As Jacob turned to his right to look at Bert, Rourke side stepped slightly to his left and as the front sight of the Python settled on the bridge of Jacob's nose… Rourke fired.

*****

Rourke put a tourniquet on Bert's arm and a field bandage on the man who had lost his finger and his revolver. He made them load the three dead in the back of the pickup and then tied them up to ride with their dead friends.

He put Jessy in the cab and tied her to the steering wheel as he took the truck keys and went back to break camp. Thirty minutes later he pulled up on the Harley and untied Jessy and told her to drive to the Fort Smith police department.

He warned her that he would be following her and would be "very disappointed" if she failed to follow instructions.

Apparently, it was not a common sight to have a pickup truck with three dead men and two wounded ones pull up to the police station, as a crowd gathered very quickly.

Jessy said the man that had shot everybody was following her, but he never showed up and, well… sometimes law enforcement in Arkansas is better left to the folks that live there. The five men were considered bullies and thugs; three of them were dead and two were arrested.

Jessy wasn't really a bad person just "a little not so right in the head" as they say in Fort Smith. No one ever knew the name of the man that had done the shooting so the Police Chief, Jessy's uncle, decided "All's well that ends well."

Chapter Forty-Six

Days later, John Thomas Rourke arrived late in the evening and, after passing the perimeter guard, parked in front of the caverns and went to the Communication Center.

He asked Master Sergeant Lancon to contact Michael and Paul and have them and their wives meet him in his quarters as soon as possible.

*****

"Welcome back," Paul Rubenstein said as John Rourke opened the door.

"Thanks, Paul. Hello Sweetheart," he said and kissed Annie on the cheek. Looking behind them he could see Michael and Natalia approaching and held the door.

Michael smiled. "Feel better, Dad?"

John shook his son's hand and hugged Natalia. "Yeah, my mind is a lot clearer. Sit down and let me tell you my plan."

Moments later, everyone was seated and John began. "We have been on the defensive. We have been playing this game with rules of political correctness. That is over. We need to go on the offensive and for the first time in a long time… we can do that."

"What do you mean, Dad?" Annie asked.

Rourke had poured coffee for Annie and some Seagram's for Michael, Natalia, Paul and himself. "Look, we thought the world had grown up and was going to play responsibly and, for about sixteen years… it did.

"But I realized on my little getaway that the world is just a crazy as it ever was. It is also just as wonderful, but there is a craziness that we can't escape. And if we can't escape it… we have to defeat it and if we can't defeat it, the result will be worse than the Night of the War.

"That war almost destroyed the physical world; it literally burned the atmosphere off… or at least a lot of it. It ripped the crust of the earth and sunk California and Florida and sent everything into a mini Ice Age. Millions, and probably billions lost their lives, the world was made over… and yet, the world survived. And, we survived but evil also survived."

"So," Michael asked, "nothing really ever changed?"

John nodded. "Not enough and what did change didn't last. What needs to change is not the world but human nature."

Paul asked, "How many times do we have to almost destroy human-kind before enough people realize how close we keep coming to that?"

"I don't know but I agree with John," Natalia said. "If anything was going to change the world, it's almost total destruction should have done it."

Annie sat listening. "So… what do you suggest we do about it?"

John took a sip of whiskey. "We have already started. We are here. We have taken steps to hide and protect the kids." He smiled then said, "Anyone, have you ever heard of the Sons of Liberty?"

"Patriots during the American Revolutionary War?" Michael asked.

John smiled. "Exactly, even then there was only a small group of American citizens willing to fight the British for freedom. Even a few years after we won our independence, the British came back and we were in the War of 1812. They burned Washington and Andy Jackson, defeated them in New Orleans and Francis Scott Key wrote the National Anthem."

"Okay, we all know the history, but I don't understand what you are proposing," Paul said.

John took another sip of whiskey. "Man's nature has not changed. Almost seven hundred years after the Night of the War, we still have Neo-Nazis, we are still fighting the Russians and we still have Globalists trying to establish a New World Order. What has changed?

"What did all of our sacrifices win for us? Sixteen, seventeen years of peace and quiet? Sixteen, seventeen years where we birthed the next generation and we did not have to shoot anyone?"

Paul frowned. "But if you are saying nothing ever changes… what do you want us to do?"

"Try," Rourke said. "We try to destroy those that are trying to destroy us. We knock down the Plantation Houses and free the slaves. We stop the Globalist and tell all mankind to rule his or her selves, the way we are supposed to. We go back to the future.

"What our forefathers designed, fought for and established, worked pretty well for a long time. Maybe nothing lasts forever and our best efforts will only get us a few generations of freedom, of peace. But that is a damned sight better than none, is it not?"

Michael interrupted, "Dad, while you were gone we received word that Beaux Delys and Tuviah Friedman have both been killed."

Rourke's jaws clamped down hard. "Do we know who got to them?"

"Yes," Michael said. "We have been able to build a link between Peter Vale and the von Arnsteins through a man named Alexander Corti, the head of their Intelligence Committee; and Demetrius Conte, head of their Continuity Committee.

"It appears that Vale is taking his orders from Conte… it is very likely that Vale has never even heard of the von Arnsteins. We also have confirmation that Andrea von Arnstein has been having reoccurring visits from the Russians; specifically one Russian by the name of Colonel Mikhail Sergeyevich."

John's eyes flashed. "The one The Keeper has told us about?"

Michael nodded. "One and the same."

"Then let's start with the Colonel and follow the bread crumbs to the rest of the rats. We are going to Russia or France or where ever we can pick up the trail of these bastards before they blow the world up… again.

"Have General Thorne plot a trip to Russia for us in The Egg, a very quiet trip; low key and under everyone's radar."

Chapter Forty-Seven

Sergeyevich left the Headquarters Building, he was still sweating. While it was true that Colonel Mikhail Sergeyevich had an ego and he was a truly duplicitous and evil bastard, he was also a consummate coward. The possibility that Ivanov had some idea about his personal involvement in a personal plan filled him with dread.

Should he have a real appraisal of what was going on... it would mean Sergeyevich's death. All Sergeyevich needed was the rest of the week; another four days. Then it would be too late for Ivanov or anyone else to threaten him.

After he left the parking lot, Sergeyevich drove to the bus station. Bus stations had probably the only pay telephones left in existence. After all, the rabble that rode on buses seldom could afford a private means of communication. He dialed the number from memory and when his call was answered, he simply said, "It is done."

He waited to hear, "Understood." As he replaced the phone receiver in its cradle, he thought he saw someone watching him. *Settle down Mikhail*, he thought. *You are seeing ghosts and monsters that don't exist.*

As Sergeyevich exited the bus station he did not see the man who had been watching him step from behind a kiosk that sold newspapers. Had he seen the man, he would have known his fear had been both real and justified.

John Thomas Rourke, wearing a fake mustache, dark glasses and work clothes moved to the window to watch Sergeyevich walk back to his car. Rourke's shoulder shifted slightly under the worn blue denim jacket as the double Alessi shoulder holster settled back into position.

The Keeper had been correct.

Chapter Forty-Eight

John Thomas Rourke, Michael Rourke and Michael's wife, Natalia, had been inside the Russian capital for two days watching and following Sergeyevich. Natalia was dressed in a moderate business ensemble with a blonde wig.

Michael Rourke sat behind the wheel of a taxi; it was a converted Russian economy car. John, Natalia, and Michael each wore an earwig microphone for communications.

"Michael," John Rourke, still in the bus station, said softly, pretending to be reading a newspaper. "Go ahead and pick up Natalia as a fare and follow our boy."

"What about you?"

"I'm going to stay here a few more minutes then I'll catch a cab and meet you back at the room. I want to see if anyone else is interested in our boy."

"Understood… I have her. See you back at the room."

John Rourke sat there for several more minutes before he saw the man. The man rose from the line of people waiting for the next bus and shuffled slowly toward the door, leaning heavily on his cane.

Rourke was positioned to be able to look out the window and see the parking lot without moving. Once the man with the cane was out of the building, his posture straightened, his stride increased and he no longer used the cane. *Got you*, Rourke thought. *But who are you?*

Rourke stood and walked quickly but nonchalantly toward the door, carrying what appeared to be a heavy duffle bag over one shoulder. Once he was outside, he saw the man being picked up by what looked to be a government sedan as all government sedans seemed to fit one description: mundane, no chrome and lacking in style. He got the license number.

Chapter Forty-Nine

Paul Rubenstein and Annie watched from a rented three bedroom hotel suite near the condominium owned by President of the United States, Phillip Greene. One of General Frank Sullivan's operatives had already tapped into Greene's cell and room phones for Paul.

The operative was listening over earphones that were plugged into a recorder and machine that maintained the tap on President Greene's communication.

He snapped his fingers and held up one hand with two fingers extended. Paul picked up the other set of earphones and listened.

"My people are pleased, Mr. President, but they are also becoming impatient," a voice said. The operative flipped several switches and a display appeared on a small screen. Two lines of audio display danced across the screen until they coalesced into one and the message, "98.7 match" appeared.

The operative slid a note across the coffee table to Paul. It read, "Peter Vale." Paul nodded.

Phillip Greene's voice stammered in his nervousness, "I cannot move things along any quicker. You must get your people to understand. That is not the way things are done in government service…"

Vale interrupted, his voice hard and low. "No. You need to understand that government service is changing and you will either change with it or we will get someone else to sit in your chair. Remember Mr. Greene, your predecessor was eliminated. Do you think we can't do that again?"

Vale smiled. Michael Rourke's accidental death due to the gas leak had given him a lot of latitude in taking credit for the tragedy.

Greene stammered again. "No… you wouldn't. I'm trying…"

"Try harder, Mr. President. Remember it was not just your predecessor… it was his whole family."

My God, Greene thought. *He did it, he killed them all. He will kill me and my wife… he killed them all.*

Then like flipping a switch, Vale changed tactics… "Mr. President, we don't need to be having a conversation like this. Not you and me. I know you understand and I know that you agree with me how… important all of this is to the country, to the world for that matter."

"I do… I do…" Greene said.

Vale interrupted again, "Then make it happen, Mr. President. My superiors want to see a joint resolution submitted to Congress for a constitutional amendment that places the sovereignty of the United States in the hands of the multinational organization currently controlling the rest of the governments on the planet.

"Such a resolution normally would require a two-thirds affirmative vote in each house but would not be submitted to the president, and would become effective when ratified by three-quarters of the States.

"Due to the extreme seriousness of the current circumstances, we expect you to present this resolution yourself, thereby adding to both its legitimacy and its immediate passage into law. Otherwise, I fear our working relationship must be terminated with extreme prejudice."

Greene was sweating profusely and spit was dribbling out of the corner of his mouth where that bastard, Michael Rourke, had elbowed him so long ago.

"Give me until the end of the month; that is only two weeks…" Greene begged.

"You have one week from today, Mr. President."

*****

In the days after the attack by Russian and KI forces, changes to government across the planet had been quick and deadly.

Changes in the heads of the FBI, Departments of Justice, State, Defense, and Homeland Security had been swift and engineered by operatives from the extremely liberal House of Representatives.

It was being openly speculated that the only reason Michael Rourke had not been impeached was he had died in office. It was no longer considered a priority to push for the impeachment of a dead man. However, other members of his administration had not been so lucky.

It had been long assumed by the general public that the military and law enforcement would always stand to protect the citizenry from even an oppressive government.

This warm and comfortable myth had been dismissed within three weeks of the attack. It was not so much the opposition was that powerful... however, the control of the media made it appear so.

Expanding on several collegiate studies of the Twentieth Century involving power and perceived power, the shift of balance required even less bloodshed than had been anticipated.

There is an old axiom that asks, "Can you shoot your own dog?" It doesn't say, "Do you want to..." it asked, could you? And it didn't ask can you shoot all of the dogs, it simply presupposed if you should shoot the "right" dog, the rest of the pack would submit. It was correct. Not many "dogs" had to be shot before the rest understood their options.

There was another "male" myth that was proven wrong. Most men legitimately believed they would do the "right" thing even when threatened with physical violence. In fact, many would do just exactly that.

But history is a brutal teacher and when only brutes study history, only brutes get to write history.

Threaten a man, he will stand fast. Put a gun in the mouth of his seven-year-old daughter and more often than not, that same man will capitulate. How could you live with yourself if you did not?

But sane men do not contemplate such insanity. Good, decent, well-educated men and women do not contemplate such insanity because it is their very goodness and decency that causes them to be so completely incapable of believing that someone or something they have voted for, or approved of, could be so completely evil.

And that is how evil has always worked, sometimes it is called terror and sometimes it is called progressivism... regardless, the end result is the same... slavery and death.

Chapter Fifty

John Rourke had followed the man to a nondescript apartment building on the outskirts of Moscow. It had a front entrance in the center of the building that led to a stairway going up three flights.

On each floor were two three-room apartments on either side of the stairs and an efficiency apartment between them. Along the rear of the building at each floor was a rusty gantry that terminated in a ladder that dropped to the ground. As Rourke studied this fire escape, he felt he was being watched from one of the apartments above.

Along this section of the street were several buildings identical to this one. Workers and their families, often large families, were crammed into these apartments in order to be close to the factory they worked in.

Behind the row of apartment buildings ran an alley, just wide enough for a small garbage truck to pass once a week for pickup.

Rourke stood two doors down in the cold of the Russian night. The smell of coal stoves warming the apartments assailed his senses; in the distance, several dogs fought over food or territory or maybe just a bitch.

"Who are you? Why do you watch me?"

The man, whoever he might be, was good; Rourke had not heard him approach. He was smart also, the man spoke English... heavily accented but English, not Russian. Rourke turned toward the voice.

Behind him, another voice said, "You heard him. Who are you and what do you want?"

Rourke finally made the accent—French with an Eastern European flavor. Rourke answered in a similar accent. "I am just getting out of the wind before I continue to my home. I wanted a cigarette, would you join me?"

Yet a third voice came out of the darkness. "Yes, Dr. Rourke, I believe we will join you. Stand very still, I have heard much about your skill with those Detonics .45s. Take them, Vassily."

Rough hands grabbed Rourke's collar and in one motion ripped the coat off of John's shoulders and down to his waist, popping off three buttons in the process.

The man called Vassily pulled first one CombatMaster and then the other from the double Alessi shoulder harness. Rourke flipped the coat back up over his shoulders. "Vassily, be careful with those. I'll need them back in a moment or two."

Vassily's accent was even deeper; he laughed. "That is too bad little man; I will not give them back to you."

Footsteps out of the dark sounded and the other two men appeared. One was the man Rourke had followed. He no longer needed a cane as he walked up close and looked at Rourke's face. "Who are you and why do you follow me?"

"Why... I'm just wondering who you are and who do you work for and what are you doing?"

The man smirked. "My name is not important but the names of my employers are and what I am doing here is also."

No one seemed to object when Rourke reached for one of his thin dark cigars, in fact, the other three produced cigarettes. Rourke snapped the cover back on the battered Zippo and in its light memorized the faces of the men as he lit their cigarettes.

Then he lit his own cigar. "Are you going to tell me?"

The man he had followed smiled amiably. "Why not? We will have a smoke, share some conversation. Have some vodka if you like..." He produced a flask.

Rourke smiled. "Thanks but I prefer whiskey."

"Sorry, we have only vodka... we will drink and talk and then kill you." He smiled and took a swig from the flask.

"As I said, my name is unimportant. We work for Roderick von Arnstein and his sister as... what is the word? Fixers, that is it; we fix things that are broken for the von Arnsteins." He laughed. "Sometimes, like this time... we just break things that are inconvenient; like you. We thought you were dead, why were you following me?"

Rourke slid his left hand through the slit in his coat pocket and cradled the Fighting Bowie in his left hand ready to draw it. "I know the von Arnsteins are trying to pull off some kind of new worldwide government."

That startled the man Rourke had been following; he threw his cigarette down and with his right hand pulled a 9mm automatic. "Kill him, kill him now."

Rourke flipped the cigar into the gunman's eyes and kicked him in the crotch as he drew the Bowie. He slapped the main edge of the Bowie across the back of the man's right hand breaking two metacarpals in the process, laying open the skin and sending the 9mm clattering.

With his own right hand, Rourke grabbed the man's arm and bringing the sharpened clip point of the Bowie back to vertical, slicing through the tendons and blood vessels of the man's right wrist and then spun to his right.

Reversing direction, Rourke grabbed the man's collar and jerked. Rourke's own momentum moved the man off balance and he fell into the other two henchmen as Rourke kept moving.

Turning as his loosed his grip on the man's collar, Rourke let the man fall and then reversed directions slamming his left elbow into Vassily's throat, crushing the man's larynx.

Rourke raised his left leg and pulled the A.G. Russell Sting 1A from his boot, slammed his left foot into the third man's knee, dislocating it.

As the man fell forward, Rourke ripped the Sting along the man's exposed throat, severing his windpipe and opening his left carotid artery.

The man tried to scream but the sounds just could not come out correctly from his destroyed throat. Vassily still laid gasping and wheezing and struggling for a breath... a breath that would not... could not come through his crushed windpipe.

A shot rang out, the slug slammed into Rourke's side, sliding painfully along his ribcage. The first man had retrieved the dropped 9mm and was shooting at Rourke using his left hand.

Rourke dropped down, spinning as he performed a leg swipe; the shooter lost his footing... two rounds flew skyward.

Rourke landed on the shooter, pinning him down as he sliced the small boot knife into the man's elbow. The sharpened double edge destroyed the ulna nerve and as an added benefit... sliced through the brachial artery. The 9mm clattered on the pavement and blood continued to spurt from severed arteries in both of the man's arms as he struggled.

"Why..." the man asked again through clenched teeth.

John Rourke asked, "What were you doing for the von Arnsteins?"

The blood loss was affecting the man's ability to process the question. "We... we were to kill... kill Colonel Mikhail Sergeyevich. He has become too much... too much of a liability for our plan to succeed."

"What plan?" Rourke hissed.

"Take control of all of the KI's operational fighters, remove all available KI technology and destroy the KI Armada in orbit."

"How were you to destroy the Armada in orbit?"

"We... we have placed...Colonel Sergeyevich's men have been placing devices on each of the KI vessels." The bleeding man no longer struggled. "Once we have everything required and have left the Armada... boom." The man smiled... he smiled and said again, "Boom."

He closed his eyes and took one last stuttering breath and died. In the distance, Rourke could hear sirens, it was time to leave. He grabbed the fallen 9mm and started to stand, as he pushed on the dead man's chest for leverage, the air from that last stuttering breath escaped in a whoosh.

Rourke retrieved his Detonics CombatMaster, turned the blood-soaked coat inside out and walked calmly out of the alley.

He went to the room he was sharing with Michael and Natalia. "We must leave now."

Michael asked, "Are you being followed?"

"No," Rourke said, "there are still bombs on the rest of the Ki Armada's ships. All of them. We must warn The Keeper. Send the signal for General Thorne to pick us up as soon as possible."

Chapter Fifty-One

Otto Croenberg had a habit of perusing obscure news reports even while in a limited form of exile guarding the Rourke and Rubenstein children. It was stories with common or related factors such as unexplained or unusual deaths that caught his attention.

That is how he became aware of Tuviah Friedman's demise. Tuviah's name was not mentioned but photos taken at the scene, while not showing his face... did show his pipe and Otto recognized it and knew the truth.

He frowned, one death was an incident; two deaths that were unrelated could be a coincidence. Two deaths of two people he had worked with to find out about the members of a super-secret group promoting a New World Order... not incidents and not coincidence.

These were surgical hits on known targets and he was now one of the targets.

He could see Beaux's death more easily than Tuviah's. Beaux, while a professional, did not have Tuviah's years of experience. While he had street smarts, tracking Neo-Nazis required more finesse; Tuviah had it but Beaux Delys... finesse was not his forte.

He hoped that his security had not been breached and that his current identity was only known to those in the Rourke camp. If he was wrong it could mean his death and the death of all of those that depended on him.

A knock at his door startled him.

Taking a Walther PPK from under a couch cushion, he walked to the door. Glancing through the peephole he relaxed, Sarah. He smiled and opened the door.

"Aren't you ready yet?"

Otto glanced at his watch, it was still almost an hour before they had to leave to get to the John Thomas Rourke Survivalist campus. "Well, I'm ready but we don't have to leave yet."

"Good," Sarah smiled and bounced into his room. "Then we can visit until we have to leave."

Otto smiled and looked past her into the hallway and said, "Why don't you come in, then?"

Sarah giggled. "I did come in, silly."

Otto smiled again. *Sarah giggled...* he thought to himself.

"How old are you, Otto?"

"Huh?"

"How old are you?"

Otto smiled. "How old do I have to be?"

"Do you know how old I am?"

"Not exactly, but I know you are a lot older than me."

Sarah smiled. "Too old for you, Mr. Croenberg?"

Otto could feel his heart race and was certain his face had to be beaming red. "I beg your pardon?"

Sarah flounced on the couch, folding her feet under her like a teenager. "Well, I have been thinking about what you said."

"What I said about what?" His face felt on fire.

She smiled coyly. "Let me see if I can quote. You stammered that you had spoken with John and then clarified that John had actually spoken with you. Then I asked what you and John had talked about and you said, 'About what we should do.'

"And I asked, 'do about what' and you said, '... the children' and I asked, 'what children' and you said, 'John's, Paul's and Michael's children.'"

Otto found his voice and said, "And I told you that John told me I will have charge and responsibility for the majority of what he values in this world and loves most in the world."

"And what did you say?"

"I said, 'I know,'" Croenberg said softly.

"And what did I say?"

"You said, 'Then I will say, good talk and good night.'"

"Correct, what else?"

"You said nothing else but you kissed me."

"Very good Mr. Croenberg." Sarah smiled and giggled. "I just wanted to make sure you didn't miss anything. See you on the bus." She turned to walk out then turned back and kissed him on the cheek.

He stood just looking at the door for a long time, feeling the kiss.

Chapter Fifty-Two

The KI Commander known as Crenshaw walked to the sliding doorway behind which The Creator had vanished. He stood there looking at the door, not sure why.

As he turned to leave, the door slid upward and The Creator walked through. He held out one hand and in it was the silver headband. Crenshaw took it and placed it on his head as he had watched Kuriname do.

Why... were... you... standing... here?

Commander Crenshaw's deep baritone voice echoed through the tunnel. "I was wondering about how to deal with you. You are not what I expected.

What... did... you... expect?

"I am not sure, but whatever it was... it was not what I have found. Your people and my people have been enemies forever."

Nothing... is... forever.

"Your people and my people have been enemies for a long, long time."

How... can... we... be... enemies... when... we... know... not... each... other?

"Our people fought a war against each other. That makes us enemies."

The Creator stood impassively staring at Commander Crenshaw, the only movement was the head which periodically moved from side to side; on a human, it could have been interpreted as quizzical or thoughtful. I... could... feel... your... thoughts... I... did... not... feel... hate.

"What did you feel?" Crenshaw asked.

You... are... curious... as... I... am. I... think... there... is... much... to... learn... from... each... other... and... much... of... what...

we... think... we... know... about... the... other... is... not... accurate... or... true.

Chapter Fifty-Three

I edged left, my eyes watching Karamatsov's eyes, the fog starting to lift and swirl as the wind picked up, sunlight breaking through. I squint, despite the glasses, against the glare of the sun on the gray fog.

It was misleading, I thought, *to say you should watch the eyes. Karamatsov had probably assumed as much. At twenty-five yards or so, the eyes themselves would be hard or impossible to see, clearly. Instead, you watched the set of the eyes,* he thought, *the almost imperceptible tightening of the muscles around them, the little squint that—*

I see his eyes set.

Karamatsov's right hand flashed up toward the Model 59 in the shoulder rig, the thumb snap breaking with an almost audible click, the gun's muzzle straightening out as Karamatsov took a half-step right and crouched, his left hand moving to help grasp the gun; the hat caught up by a gust of wind and sailing from his head.

My right hand moves first, then my left, the right hand bringing the first Detonics on line; the safety swept off under my thumb as the gun cleared the leather, the gun in the left hand moving on line as I trigger the first shot.

I see the flash against the fog of Karamatsov's pistol, the stainless Detonics bucking through recoil in my right hand, then the left gun firing, then the right and the left simultaneously.

Karamatsov flew up off the ground almost a foot, I judge, the gun in Karamatsov's hands firing up into the air—a second round. The Russian's body twitches in midair, then lurches twice more as it falls, the Russian's gun firing again into the street. A window smashes on the other side. His body rolls over face down, the right arm and left leg twitching, shivering, and then stopping.

There was no more movement.

I thumb up the safety on the pistol in my right hand and jab it into my belt, shifting the gun in my left hand to my right, thumb up the safety and hold the gun limp at my side against my thigh and walk forward, slowly, then stop, rolling over the Russian's body with my combat-booted foot, my right thumb poised over the safety of the pistol.

There are four dark-red patches on Karamatsov's trunk.

I bend over and, with the thumb of my left hand, close the eyelids.

"Done," I whisper.

*****

Paul Rubenstein sat on a chair by Rourke's bed. He had heard Rourke shouting in his sleep and woke his friend. Rourke wiped his face with both hands and sat up on the bed.

"And for over five centuries I believed that I had killed the bastard."

"But that was not to be, was it?" Paul Rubenstein said. "You went to sleep for five hundred years and woke up to find your enemy waiting for you?"

Rourke nodded. "Pretty much, frankly I'm still not sure how he survived four .45 caliber rounds to the chest… but he did and he and I would dance several more times but on the last one…" Rourke drew strangely quiet for a long moment.

"Vladmir Karamatsov and I were fighting on the edge of a precipice above the sea. We were exhausted. He staggered to his feet and suddenly the little snub-nosed Smith and Wesson .38 he had carried five centuries before appeared in his right hand. 'You're dead, John Rourke,' he said. I was helpless but I was also committed to rushing him in a headlong tackle that would see us both over the edge to the rocks below. Anything was preferable to him going free.

"Suddenly Natalia appeared next to him and shouted, 'No Vladmir!' She held the short-sword-sized Life Support System X knife in her hands. The blade flashed up over her head and around in an arc to her right… then the Crain knife stopped moving.

"Karamatsov's body swayed and as the little revolver fell from his limp right hand… his head separated from his neck and sailed outward into the wind. A bloody geyser sprayed into the air and the headless torso of her husband rocked backwards and fell into the rocks and sea below."

Looking around the otherwise empty bedroom, he said, "I do not know who is behind the Russian conspiracy; it can't be Karamatsov. I killed him once myself and then Natalia killed him again and that death was forever."

Chapter Fifty-Four

Paul shook his head in wonder. "So, the Third Chinese City is both a legend and a fact?"

Morrell nodded and Mid-Wake's Grand Archivist, Steven Delervello said, "I think it is real; further I think that is where we will find what is left of Karamatsov and Rozhdestvenskiy's nest of KGB bastards. Some intelligence seems to indicate reports of obscure groups of lost Taoist and Russians somewhere along the Sino-Russian border. I suspect that what happened is an alliance of some form was developed between Karamatsov and some of the Taoist monks before The Night of the War.

"We know secret preparations for three special Chinese Cities began in the 1950s. Rather than being actual cities, they were more like secret military bases... very unusual secret military bases. To the rest of the world, China under Mao Zedong, and Russia under several prime ministers, were at odds with each other... even were enemies. However, there were undercurrents of cooperation particularly between a rather 'militant' group of Taoist priests and the KGB."

"Taoism was supposed to be a religion or something, wasn't it?" Paul asked.

Morrell nodded. "In its true and pure application, Taoism is a religious or philosophical tradition of living in harmony with the Tao or 'the way.' Taoism focuses on the principle that is the source, pattern and substance of everything that exists and differs from Confucianism by not emphasizing rigid rituals and social order, but is similar in the sense that it is a teaching about the various disciplines for achieving 'perfection' by becoming one with the unplanned rhythms of the universe called 'the way.'

"Taoist ethics vary depending on the particular school, but in general tend to emphasize action without intention, 'naturalness,' simplicity, spontaneity, and the Three Treasures: compassion, frugality, and humility."

Delervello added, "Female shamans played an important role in this tradition, which was particularly strong in the southern states of China. It is these female shamans that I think held the key to the secret of the Third Chinese City."

"Rozhdestvenskiy and Karamatsov were both sadistic chauvinist S.O.B.s; you're suggesting they aligned with female shamans?" Paul asked.

"They were also charismatic, sadistic, chauvinist S.O.B.s. After all, Karamatsov had convinced Natalia to marry him, remember?" Delervello reminded.

Chapter Fifty-Five

Akiro Kuriname was piloting The Egg craft. John Thomas Rourke sat alone with his thoughts watching the holographic screen in front of the control panel. "John, are you sure you want to do this alone?" Rourke sat without answering. "John…"

"I heard you, Akiro." Rourke stretched his back. "First of all, if I am correct in my hypothesis… I don't believe there is a high danger threat. Secondly, I need to get back in the field. This sitting around watching everyone else that has a mission is killing me."

"But, by yourself…"

"Akiro, truth be told I have been by myself most of my adult life in one way or another. It is a terrible thing to admit but my time with the CIA when I was in danger, the times after the Night of the War, the times when we all were closest to death… those are the times I felt most alive."

"Except when you awoke to help Michael and Annie…"

Thoughtfully, Rourke smiled. "Yes, that was the exception. It truly was a wonderful time." Shaking himself, Rourke turned. "Look, just stick with the schedule and be here on time to pick me up. I'll be fine."

*****

The Egg materialized long enough to discharge its passenger, John Rourke. Kuriname activated the counter-illuminated camouflage that created an invisibility cloak or a force field, assuming the colors and textures of its surroundings; this time the sky. An instant later, Rourke was alone on the plains of China.

He shouldered his backpack, took a compass reading and started walking. After an hour, he stopped. He dropped his pack, took a sip from his canteen and scanned the area with his binoculars. Removing the handkerchief from around his neck, he took off his sunglasses and wiped his face. As he retied the handkerchief, he felt eyes on him… it was almost a physical thing.

Chapter Fifty-Six

He walked… it seemed like forever he had been walking. He realized how long it had really been since he had entered a quest like this. Back… back before the children, he realized. Certainly there had been adventures after them, especially in the days after the Night of the War, but not like before. He looked at the horizon; he would have to make camp soon.

He still was not sure how he would make contact… he was not even sure if there was someone to make contact with. But his gut had told him there was and he had to know for sure. He adjusted his backpack and removed his aviator sunglasses and wiped his face on his handkerchief. He stopped, turned his head slowly to the left while keeping his eyes focused on the spot.

He smiled. Off in the distance behind the next line of ridges, he had seen a reflection. Not high on the side of a ridge, nor was it a reflection as if off of glass or water. This was very probably the only spot on this high plain where it could have been seen because it was behind the next ridges. He was sure he had found it, by mid-morning tomorrow he would know if he was correct or not.

He picked a spot near the horizon where he would spend the night and started off.

*****

He stopped at a small stream and refilled his canteens and decided to go further than he had originally planned. The lay of the land was gentle and easy and he was making excellent time. A good night's sleep with an early rise and he would see his goal before lunch.

He picked a spot that would give him some shelter from the wind and protection should he need it. He stripped the backpack and removed the old CAR 15 rifle from its straps. He built a fire ring out of rocks and found enough dry wood to last through the night then pitched his tent, finishing as the sun started to set.

After a pot of stew, he cleaned his dishes. Leaning next to a boulder, he pulled a thin dark cigar from his pack and rolled the striker wheel on his battered Zippo lighter touching the yellow blue flame to the cigar and puffing. He inhaled deeply and slowly exhaled the smoke, watching it swirl on the evening breeze. He reached into a side pocket on his pack and removed a flask filled with Seagram's and leaned back against the bolder.

The stars were brilliant in the night sky once the sun had set. There was no moon but the starlight alone was sufficient to see into the night. He saw a Gecko scurry up to the foot of the boulder before it saw him. Offended to find another creature in his territory, the Gecko vocalized his displeasure with a variety of chirps, squeaks, and clicking sounds. From somewhere in the deep regions of his mind, Rourke remembered that the chirping was used to define territory and also as a mating call.

Rourke held the flask up in a peace-making toast, "Here's to you little guy. Look around at this night. You get to see it every night but my species seldom even goes outside at night anymore. This is definitely the way to live. In fact, I might just move in with you." A series of chirps, squeaks, and clicking sounds broke the still of the evening and Rourke smiled at what he took to be a protest. He saluted the lizard one last time and then said, "Okay, I'll stay with my people and you stay with yours."

Chapter Fifty-Seven

He woke just before dawn and urinated behind one of the boulders and then started to break camp. Twenty minutes later he was on the move. He hadn't wanted to spend the time to make coffee and was beginning to regret that decision when he saw the first signs of a pathway.

He was getting closer.

He stopped and weighed his options and decided to secure the CAR 15 to his pack and proceed with the Detonics CombatMasters hidden under his bomber jacket. "More politically correct," he said aloud.

Twenty feet later as he rounded a line of boulders, he wished he could rethink his position. But it was too late, before him stood a line of men, twelve in all. They were mounted on twelve of the short Mongol horses common to this area. Rourke stopped walking and smiled, keeping his hands out to his sides, not in surrender but to show he was not a threat. It was then that he noticed the thirteenth horse.

*****

They rode the rest of the way through a winding path of rocks and boulders and ridges and it was not long before Rourke had no sensation of distance or time. Suddenly, there came the sound of a gong... a very large gong. Around the next bend of the trail was a sight that Rourke was not prepared for.

There was a gate that had been cut and carved into the cliff face. It reminded Rourke of Petra in Jordan which was carved out of living sandstone. It was one of the most remarkable things Rourke ever saw.

The capital of the Nabataean Empire between 400 B.C. and A.D. 106, Petra had been lost to the western world until the 1800s.

If Petra still existed, it was older than this site but Rourke decided that this one was even grander. For one thing, this cliff looked to be solid granite, not sandstone and whereas Petra was hidden in a narrow canyon, this city was hidden behind a network of ridges that almost blocked every view of this gate.

Scanning the crowd that had gathered to welcome him, Rourke saw women and children that were smiling and grinning at him. He saw men that were watching him but not in a threatening manner. Then he saw something that was extremely threatening. Near the back of the group on the left side was a man in black. Not black robes or pantaloons but the black tunic and britches of the Russian KGB.

Surreptitiously Rourke checked the small compass he had brought. This obviously was the south gate to the city. While it was a city it was almost certainly a Taoist Temple and, as such, guests would be required to enter from the southern entrance and exit through the northern entrance.

Rourke noticed vendors; one common custom when visiting a holy Chinese site is to purchase a bundle of incense. These are usually sold just outside temples. Visitors may purchase a package of incense, light these items and hold them in both hands while they pray. There are often incense holders where worshipers can place their incense once they have finished praying.

One of the riders who had escorted him dismounted and walked up to Rourke's horse. Waving with one hand the rider indicated Rourke should dismount and follow him. Rourke did so and followed the man up the steps that had been carved into the granite wall and through the gate.

Chapter Fifty-Eight

Rourke was led into a large and ornate chamber room. Several large bronze braziers gave off a soft but illuminating light while huge incense burners as large as the braziers filled the room with a pleasant cacophony of aromas. In the middle of the room, on a structure that might be called a dais, stood something similar to a gazebo. And in the gazebo stood a large and ornate throne, and on the throne sat a creature of incredible poise and grace and beauty.

She was a figure from the ancient Chinese Empire both in dress and demeanor, but the real surprise came when she spoke saying, "Welcome to our city" in perfect English. "You and I shall meet informally later, but for now I have been asked to tell you the rules and boundaries of our city for this is not only our physical home, it is our temple. This hall you are in may be called the Gong, Guan or Miao in Chinese. It is where we Taoists perform our religious ceremonies.

"Unlike your people, we have many deities that you might correspond to gods. Throughout the city are several temples with different gods. Should you wish to pray for your work or relationships or fortune, or even health, there are different temples for each of them. Make sure to decide what you want to pray for and which temple you're planning to go to and your escort shall make sure you arrive.

"You might wish to bring flowers, fruits, drinks, or food to worship the god of your chosen temple. There will be vendors around to sell these offering. Fruit and flowers are common offerings as well as food but remember that some offerings require homophonic words to have the correct connection with the correct god."

Rourke was enthralled by her; he had often heard of the allure of the oriental woman and had even met several during his days as a CIA operative... but never anyone like this.

Chapter Fifty-Nine

Paul Rubenstein was returning to Retreat 2. It felt good to be back on his Harley. The weather was decent and although, "as a crow flies," it was less than fifteen miles to the Underground complex, the trip down had taken two hours.

Two hours to find a pathway through the cracked and tumbled roadways and debris from collapsed bridges and buildings. James White, the "mayor" of the Underground, had offered for Paul to stay overnight since the hour was late. Paul had declined, opting to spend the night with Annie in Retreat 2 rather than in the Underground.

While White and his people were all pleasant ... Paul couldn't put his finger on it but the place and the people gave him the creeps, with the exception of Lane Alexander and his son Noah.

The old town of Springfield, Missouri had been decimated during the first barrage of missiles the day the Russians had launched. Following that, the geologic slippages around the country as fault lines opened up and changed the terrain forever; not to mention the atmosphere catching fire and then the resultant nuclear winter. After almost seven centuries it was difficult to determine what the layout of Springfield had ever been.

He was roughly following an old road map Lane Alexander had given him. From the Underground, he had traveled west for just a few minutes and was on what used to be Highway 65 North. He knew the on ramps that would put him on the old I-44 West had collapsed so after a few minutes, he veered off of 65 North to go cross country a mile or so before trying to get on I-44.

The big Harley was definitely not a common dirt bike but then Paul Rubenstein was not a common rider. He and John Rourke had traversed more difficult terrain that this in their search for Sarah Rourke and the kids.

The kids… it still amazed Paul that he had two completely different concepts of Michael and Annie Rourke. The first was the children they were when he first met them. Michael a smaller version of John Rourke, less serious but not by much, and less confident but he grew out of that. Annie was so small, but she grew to have the confidence and abilities of both her mother and her father.

And upon reawakening, Paul was pleased to find that John Rourke had awakened the kids before the rest of them for the training and education they would need to survive. When he had awakened, instead of this little girl he remembered, she was now a young lady. A beautiful young lady and his view of her had not changed after all of these years.

He slowed the bike. *What is that up ahead*, he wondered. Unconsciously, he snuggled the Schmeisser closer to him. A large tree had fallen and was blocking the highway and it was blocking it at a bridge that spanned a drop off… *Now, isn't that inconvenient? And the tree is not a dead tree that blew over or finally its roots gave away. Someone felled that tree to block this particular road at this particular time. TRAP!* Rubenstein cut hard left toward the median and gunned the big bike forward.

Suddenly, gunfire erupted… *AMBUSH!* Rourke's training kicked in, *Go… Go… Go! Get out of the kill zone. Get out of range of any grenades and weapons, go… go… go!* He shouted in his mind as he downshifted.

When he cleared the median, he jerked the Schmeisser around. Gunfire was coming from the right side of the road and Rubenstein squeezed off several quick bursts with his left hand while he kept the throttle wide open with his right. He looked up ahead, the path seemed clear if he stayed on the highway.

Off to his right, he spotted a game trail that went off toward what remained of an old subdivision. Something in his head shouted, *Take that*... Without hesitation, he grabbed the rear brake, turned the handlebars and leaned. The Harley left the pavement and as it did Paul stood on the footrest with bent knees to take the impact. A glance over his shoulder told him he had made the right choice.

People were filing out of the ambush zone on both sides of the road; he guessed there were at least fifteen. Ducking low in the saddle, Paul kicked the bike up a gear and kept the throttle open. Had he stayed on the highway, he would already have been killed. Rourke always told him, "Have a plan, but listen to your gut." In his rearview mirror, he spotted people running after him.

Chapter Sixty

Rourke had been summoned. An entourage consisting of six armed male warriors and six unarmed female maidens led him into the chamber in which he had been greeted before by the woman. The last to enter the chamber was the most remarkable, it was her.

Standing now, Rourke could tell she was tall, taller than the other women. Her luxurious black hair had been coiffured by her handmaidens; the long tresses piled luxuriously on her head and pinned. He doubted her hair had ever been cut and guessed it would have touched the floor.

Her skin was almost a pale gold, but it was her eyes that held the attention of all who met her; they were green. Green eye color is the rarest color found around the world, and it is estimated that only around two percent of the world's population has green colored eyes. Green eye color is a result of a mild amount of pigmentation in the eye with a golden tint... or it may simply be the result of magic, who could say. Her nails were long and painted, her lips dark and sensual... she did not walk across the floor... she floated.

"I am wu," she said simply; her English held but a tint of an accent. To say she was beautiful was an understatement of the highest order. "That is not who I am but what I am, it is my Taoist title. I am what you would call a shaman." Rourke nodded his understanding.

"In the *shamanic* religious tradition of Wuism, since the late Zhou dynasty, 1045 to 256 BCE, the word wu has been used to specify the *'female shaman or* sorceress' as opposed to word xi used to describe the male *shaman or* sorcerer.

"The history of female shamanism was erased from the world's history long ago. Yet, even from ancient history to modern times, particularly in the Orient, female shamans have predominated in art, ritual culture, classical literature, historical records, and temple worship."

"Why have I never heard of this?" Rourke asked.

Without anger or even haughtiness, she smiled. "Does your ignorance or bias change facts you were unaware of? My sisters and I, those of us that are practicing Wu, perform invocations, divinations, interpret dreams, heal, drive off evil spirits in exorcisms and we dance. We perform ecstatic rain dances, we are... you see, ecstasy in flesh. When we dance we become invisible, we slash ourselves with knives and swords, cut our tongues, swallow swords, and spit fire.

"Our whirling dances also allow us to speak the language of the spirits and make objects rise in the air and fly about. Then we are often carried off onto a cloud that shines as if lit by lightning. One of my sisters sings how, 'We rise to heaven and brush away the comets.' Even the written character for wu depicts shamans dancing around a pillar, or the long sleeves of a shaman's robe swirling as she dances."

"How are you called? How should I address you?" he asked.

"As I am unmarried, you may choose. You may call me Lady Wu or Mistress Wu... either will suffice for a formal title. Jiang Ying Yue is my personal name. It translates to 'river reflection of the moon.' Jiang is my surname or family name, of course."

"Of course, it is a lovely name for a lovely lady."

She smiled slightly and he barely perceived the bow of her head.

"Now... what or how shall address you?"

"Lady Wu, my name is John Rourke. My formal title is Doctor."

For an instant he thought he saw something in her eyes. Her voice was still soft and musical when she said, "Doctor John Thomas Rourke?" He had been correct; there had been something he saw in her eyes. When he nodded, she raised her right hand and extended her index finger.

Before he could react, the six armed male warriors had moved to surround him. He stood perfectly still for a long moment. "Lady Wu, I mean you and your people no harm, I assure you."

"What about my people?" a voice behind him shouted.

Slowly, carefully, Rourke turned and saw a man he did not recognize in a uniform he did recognize. It was the black dress uniform of the Russian KGB. The same uniform Karamatsov and Rozhdestvenskiy had worn so long ago. Slowly and carefully Rourke turned back to face Lady Wu. "Lady Wu, I mean you and your peo..."

Something struck him hard in the back of his head; suddenly he was sure he could see Lady Wu on a cloud that was shining as if lit by lightning... Then everything went dark.

Chapter Sixty-One

When consciousness returned, it did so both slowly and painfully. Lightning had moved from the cloud Lady Wu floated on to inside his head where it ricocheted around painfully. Keeping his eyes closed, Rourke assessed his situation. His arms and legs were restrained. There was an additional strap across his chest but he seemed to be uninjured except for the headache.

"Well, Dr. Rourke... as they say, 'Welcome back to the land of the living.'" Rourke opened his eyes; he was lashed to a medical gurney. "I have to admit, Dr. Rourke... while I never conceived of actually meeting you, I am rather excited to have done so. I have heard much about you and the days before The Night of the War. I hope to learn more from you."

Painfully turning his head to the left and squinting, Rourke saw the man that had addressed him earlier... just before the lights went out. He still wore the uniform and it had the rank of a Russian Naval Captain 1st Class; Rourke thought it was unusual for a KGB operative to be Navy. It was the equivalent rank to a Russian Army or Air Force Colonel.

Rourke questioned simply, "Captain..."

Clicking his heels like the Cossack fighters he admired so much... "Captain Vadimovich Ragulin, descendent of Admiral Kostantin Grigoryevich Ragulin, Russian Submarine Command. My ancestor was part of a secret mission just days before the Night of the War.

"On June 30, 1976, the keel was laid for the Dmitriy Donskoy, a Russian Navy nuclear ballistic missile submarine. It was an Akula class, or as NATO would refer to it... a Typhoon class submarine, one of the largest submarines in the world. It was launched in September of 1980 on a secret mission that resulted in what you now see before you.

"It was powered by two OK-650 nuclear reactors and when fully armed would have carried twenty of the Bulava SLMs or submarine-launched ballistic missiles. Each single missile was capable of striking several targets. Additionally, it had four twenty-one-inch torpedo tubes and two twenty-six-inch torpedo tubes. After it deposited my ancestor and his men at this location, the Donskoy returned to open water to be commissioned after further sea trials. It is speculation, but I assume the Night of the War occurred before the commissioning ceremony as I have no record of it."

Ragulin walked over to the gurney and pulled a pin from the frame and swung Rourke upright, almost in a standing position but still secured to the gurney. Looking Rourke in the eye, Ragulin asked with a smile, "Would you like to know what the secret mission was?"

Rourke shrugged. Ragulin's smile disappeared... "So, would I. My ancestor's instructions were to establish contact with Chinese personnel already in place and await further instructions; instructions that were never received."

Rourke shook his head. "So for all of this time... all of these genera-tions... your people have been..."

Ragulin slumped visibly. "Yes, Dr. Rourke... we have been, as you would say... 'winging it.' I had hoped you might know what the mission was. By the way, sorry for the blow on the head but I had to have you secured as quickly as possible."

Rourke nodded. "And now?"

Ragulin nodded and a sergeant came forward and undid the restraints. "And now... what difference does it make? Dr. Rourke, all my people and I know of the outside world is what we have gleaned through radio transmissions."

Rourke stepped off the gurney and rubbed his wrist. "So, you have no cryogenic chambers here and you never heard of someone named Karamatsov?"

Ragulin stiffened. "Incorrect, we have forty-three cryogenic chambers that are fully functional and I have heard of Marshall Karamatsov. He was to be in charge of the operational aspects of our mission and the mission of another such facility. But his last contact was long ago. He was supposed to return and fully activate this facility for the third phase of the mission but never did."

Rourke nodded. "I wouldn't leave out the welcome mat, Captain. Karamatsov got distracted and lost his head."

Chapter Sixty-Two

Ragulin and Rourke spoke for several hours; the conversation was disappointing for both of them. Ragulin learned some about the outside world, little of which made any sense to him. Rourke found that the Third Chinese City was not a fountain of answers or a river of threats. It was simply a pitiful example of the detritus of a world that no longer existed except in the faithful hearts of these Russians who had held on to the hopes of an unknown mission that would have at least given some purpose to their lives and those that had waited before them... waited on instructions, waited on orders... waited on answers that had never come.

Rourke's mind drifted to Shangri-La, the fictional place described in the 1933 novel *Lost Horizon* by the British author James Hilton. It was obvious that this city might be as mystical, harmonious, gently guided by a religious order, but it was not a Shangri-La. *Although*, he thought, *the people seem happy and they are certainly isolated from the world. I wonder... are they almost immortal, living hundreds of years beyond the normal lifespan and only very slowly aging in appearance?*

*****

"Tell me Captain Ragulin, you said you are a descendent of Admiral Kostantin Grigoryevich Ragulin of the Russian Submarine Command."

"Correct, Dr. Rourke."

"And I am to understand this facility was never fully activated before the Night of the War and yet, you have forty-three cryogenic chambers and sufficient serum but no one activated them before the world ended? Yet, you know of Karamatsov but he never assumed control of this city and you and the Chinese Taoist have evolved into this very unique and symbiotic relationship. Am I accurate?"

"You are."

"You consider yourself KGB?"

Ragulin's eyes flashed. "I am KGB and I have been all of my life."

Rourke frowned slightly. "Then you can tell me what the KGB is?"

"The KGB or more accurately the Komitet Gosudarstvennoy Bezopasnosti is the Committee for State Security for the Union of Soviet Socialist Republics."

Rourke said slowly, "You are aware that the Union of Soviet Socialist Republics... no longer exists aren't you?"

Captain Grigori Vadimovich Ragulin glanced down at the floor and said slowly, "I have come to realize that, yes."

Rourke took a deep breath. "You know I am former CIA, the American counterpart to the KGB, and that by itself makes us enemies, correct? You realize that the CIA that I served and the KGB that your distant relative served no longer exist, correct? You realize that several factions threaten the very survival of the world, none of which are our doings, correct?

"Correct."

Rourke grew very quiet and looked down at the floor. "Grigori, did you know I have had several very good friends that were Russian? In fact, I fell in love with a Russian KGB agent one time."

"Do not play me, Dr. Rourke..." Ragulin said.

"No, it is true; all of it but one of my friends was a Captain Vladov whom General Varakov told me was the best soldier he ever knew."

"You knew General Varakov?"

Rourke nodded. "He was the uncle of the Russian girl I once loved. Just before Captain Vladov died on a mission Varakov had sent us on, he told me a story. He said that the name of his unit was 'Bor'ba'… and in Russian it means…"

A tear ran down Ragulin's face. "In Russian, it means 'Fight.' You knew the Bor'ba men? One of my ancestors, an uncle many times removed from me, was a Bor'ba."

Rourke nodded. "Yes… I knew them, I fought with them but the point of this story is something Vladov asked me to do. He asked that if the world survived and if I survived that somewhere in that new world a street or village square be named Bor'ba so that if the human race continued… he asked for a street or village square where children could play. He believed that somehow… his people would know of that street or village square where a Russian word was in an American town. He thought that would be fitting for the human race in a new world."

Ragulin looked up at Rourke. "And did you do that, Dr. Rourke? Did you name a street or village square Bor'ba for Captain Vladov?"

"At last count, there are twenty-seven streets and town squares that carry that name including some in New Germany, Australia, and England," Rourke said, smiling.

Ragulin stood. "Then we must not be enemies, Dr. Rourke. We may not become friends; it is too early to tell. But we shall not be enemies. On that you have my word."

*****

Rourke realized that there were no longer questions to be asked. *How sad*, Rourke thought. Ragulin decided that there was no purpose for them to be enemies and it was too early for them to be friends. Captain Ragulin finally left Rourke alone in silence with instructions to return to his room. Walking down the hallway, hearing only his own boot heels making noise, Rourke was lost in thought. Later, Ragulin had said he would introduce Rourke to his men and give Rourke a tour of their facility. Right now, Rourke wanted to see the other side. Out of the corner of his eye, Rourke caught a movement off to his left and turned.

She stood in the hallway. "Lady Wu…" Rourke bowed.

She smiled. "I am not the Lady Wu at this moment, Dr. Rourke."

Rourke smiled. "Jiang Ying Yue?" She nodded and smiled. "It is nice to see you again, Yue," Rourke said and bowed again. "How may I serve you?"

"Tell me of your world, Dr. Rourke and… tell me of you."

Rourke smiled a sad smile. "A world is only what you make of it. And there is nothing left of my life worth talking about." He turned and continued walking. He did not notice a single tear roll down her golden cheek.

Chapter Sixty-Three

Jiang Ying Yue sat on an ornate stool as her handmaiden combed the long dark hair with a comb made from a tortoiseshell. "He is a very troubled man, Mian."

Feng Mian, whose name conjures up the idea of falling asleep in the woods as the breeze swishes through, smiled as she combed Yue's long tresses. "Mistress, is it that he is a troubled man or does he trouble you?"

Yue smiled, turned slightly and then lovingly smacked Mian's left buttock. They both laughed. "You know me too well, Mian." Yue's smile faded. "His heart is filled with much pain and has been for a long time. Some of the pain is brown and wilted and some of it green and new. He is a man that has not been able to live his life for himself... but for responsibilities and the pleasures and passions of the world. There is great sadness in him."

"Do not let his sadness fill you, My Lady, let your joy fill him," Mian said with a smile.

*****

For Rourke sleep would not come in spite of being tired. Exhausted as he was, the instant his head hit the pillow... his eyes flew open and his mind raced. What could he do to stop the Russians and the militant KI? What could he do to save his country? What could he do to save the world? What could he do stop the Globalist threat? What could he do to stop Emma's anguish and pain?

The air within his sleeping chamber shifted, the scent it now carried was both subtle and provocative. Gradually, the tension started to leave his body… the creases in his face relaxed, his breathing deepened… He slept, deeply for the first time in a long time.

In her quarters, Yue smiled deeply… also for the first time in a long time.

Chapter Sixty-Four

John Thomas Rourke's mind slowly stirred; he felt rested. He could not remember the last time he had slept so well.

Rourke's bladder was full and he relieved himself in the chamber pot with a heavy sigh and then opened the heavy drapes that covered the ceiling-to-floor windows. Outside the city was coming to life; vendors were opening their shops and people were already moving about their normal activities. In the parlor just outside the sleeping quarters, he found his clothes had been washed and ironed. His boots were cleaned and shined... *I could get used to this kind of treatment*, he thought. He dressed quickly; the green handled Survivalist Sting went into the inside of his left boot, ready for a right-handed draw.

The Fighting Bowie he threaded horizontally on his belt, it was ready for a left handed draw. His ancient black chrome A.G. Russell Sting 1A rested behind his right hip bone. He picked up his double Alessi shoulder rig from the floor next to the bed. He cleared each of the stainless Detonics CombatMasters and, after verifying both were ready for whatever the day held in store, returned them to the holsters and snapped the trigger guard retention snaps.

He slung the rig over his broad shoulders and gave a slight shrug to settle them in place, put on his battered brown bomber jacket and stepped out of the apartment. *Hmmm, no guards*, he thought, seeing no one standing by the door or even close to it. He decided that was a pleasant if unexpected way to start the day.

As he exited the structure his apartment was in, he noticed for the first time the underground city was lit by some form of artificial lighting. High above him in the ceiling of the huge cavern shone a light that looked like the sun. It was not an orb, round and shining... rather a uniform glow that was bright enough to cast shadows but not hurt the eyes, unless one stared at it like Rourke was doing. He squinted and looked away. He rubbed his eyes and put on his aviator sunglasses and began walking.

He had paid attention as he had been escorted to the sleeping quarters last night and in a few moments was standing close to the gates to the underground city, watching. People seemed to enter and leave the city by their own will with little interaction with the guards at the gate. Rourke decided to test the waters; he began walking toward the gate. He passed the guard and kept walking, in moments he was outside in the bright daylight.

He walked to one side of the cliff face until he was in the shade and pulled one of his thin dark cigars out. He pulled his battered Zippo from the pocket of his jeans and rolled the striker wheel. While watching the activities around him, he puffed the cigar drawing the yellow blue flame into the synthetic tobacco until he had it lit to his satisfaction. No one appeared to care about him one way or another.

"Dr. Rourke," a voice called from behind. Rourke turned to see Captain Grigori Vadimovich Ragulin approaching. "How are you this morning, Dr. Rourke?"

"Call me John."

"Call me Grigori, then." Ragulin smiled. "Now, same question, how are you this morning, Dr. Rourke?"

"Frankly, Grigori, while I feel rested I am somewhat confused."

Ragulin frowned slightly. "Confused?"

Rourke nodded and took another puff from the cigar. "Confused, pleasantly so but… yes, confused."

"Elaborate, John. Maybe I can address your confusion."

Rourke smiled. "First, I can't remember having a better night's sleep in a long time. Second, when I left the sleeping quarters I found no guards posted by my door. Third, I have walked freely around the city even to the point of exiting the city gates with no interference at all."

"First of all, the air inside the city is provided and treated to remove toxins as you sleep," Ragulin said, smiling. "Did you experience a driving need to urinate when you awoke?" Rourke nodded. "Then the system is working on you. Second, there were no guards because you are not a prisoner. Third, why interfere with your movements, where else would you go?"

"Grigori, our first meeting was, shall we say, not as friendly as this one. One of your Russians smacked me in the back of the head and I awoke strapped down on a medical gurney..." Rourke eyed the Russian. "Now, you act like you want to be..."

"Friends, John?"

"Yeah, but it is a bit difficult to follow considering our initial meeting."

"John Thomas Rourke, enemy of my country, enemy of Vladmir Karamatsov, destroyer of the Russian Womb, killer of Colonel Rozhdestvenskiy... And the list goes on, John Rourke."

"Captain Grigori Vadimovich Ragulin, enemy of my country, subordinate of Vladmir Karamatsov and Rozhdestvenskiy... does that list go on also, Grigori?"

Ragulin smiled. "Might I have one of your cigars, John? I have always wanted to share one with you."

Rourke gave Ragulin a cigar and the Zippo. After a couple of puffs, Ragulin tried to inhale and that produced a bout of coughing. Rourke smiled and said, "Takes a little getting used to if you are going to inhale."

Ragulin smiled through his tears, and inhaled again... he held it for a time then breathed the smoke out. "Ah, that is better. You see John Rourke, I have studied you since childhood. You are famous in my country or rather... infamous. But, there was something about the reports on you that always troubled me. Bothered me and did not match up with the picture I was given to believe about you."

"What?"

"General Ishmael Varakov, the leader of the Soviet Occupation Forces in America, apparently trusted you. And my ancestor, Admiral Kostantin Grigoryevich Ragulin, of the Russian Submarine Command, knew General Varakov and trusted him. So, how do I balance the picture I have of you as an enemy of my people when apparently you were friends, or at least friendly, with one of the highest ranking of my people following the Night of the War."

Rourke looked down, lost in memories for a moment. He looked up, took a drag off the cigar and deeply inhaled it. "General Varakov was not only a patriotic, honorable and reasonable Soviet soldier, he was my friend. He was also the uncle of someone I cared deeply about at that time. Someone he trusted me to save from the annihilation of humanity. To this day, my family honors General Varakov on his birthday each year."

Ragulin took another hit from the cigar and inhaled deeply. Slowly, letting the smoke out of his lungs he smiled… "I think John Rourke you are little like this smoke, a little hard to handle initially but rather nice after you get used to it."

Chapter Sixty-Five

Mayor White rose from his seat and walked to the podium. His normally confident demeanor was shaken. His eyes were red and sunken and those standing closest to him could see his hands shaking with fatigue. The mayor had not slept well for days.

"Ladies and Gentlemen, I stand before you with shame in my heart… a dark cloud has settled over us. It is a cloud of evil and ungodliness… it is a cloud I share some blame in bringing to you." The congregation hummed with muted conversations, indistinct and angry.

"The people from the outside do not wish to join us… and by not being willing to join us… they have set themselves against us. Too many times, we have watched factions from our own people separate and move away from the word, the word of God."

More rumbling came from the audience, the hushed conversations grew louder. "You know and I know that differences in opinions are normal and healthy, but there must be some constants within a group of people or that group of people cannot be healthy… they can only be divided and division eventually puts brother against brother, father against son and mother against daughter.

"We have shared our knowledge with the outsiders and, at first…" he paused for effect and coaxed tears to his eyes before continuing. "At first, it seemed they would join us, but that was a lie." Several people in the rear of the meeting hall stood as if on command and began shouting, "The Outsiders must go…" and "Push them out…" and finally, "Tell us, Mayor, what we must do…" Others in the meeting hall caught the virus of hate and joined in also. Mayor White smiled.

"It is time to call forth our Angels, for our Angels have always protected this flock… our Angels have always guarded us from evil." A chant began in the rear of the meeting hall and gained momentum: "Angels... Angels... Angels..." Across the congregation, men began standing up. They ranged from late teens to early middle age, all appeared physically fit. These were the Angels. They were the most devout, the most dedicated and the most dangerous members of the congregation.

Chapter Sixty-Six

Paul had traveled for about five minutes, he was lost. He pulled off what remained of the street and found he was alongside of a straight "through" railroad track. *Must have been the main line that ran through Springfield*, he thought. He looked for a switch, a short section of track, that allowed a train to change directions to the right or left as appropriate. A half mile up, he saw what he needed.

What remained of two railroad cars were sitting; one on the main line and the other on the switch. The angle of the switch caused one car to be offset from the other. Paul pulled between them and got off the Harley. He changed mags in the Schmeisser and pulled the communication set and a pair of binoculars out of his saddlebag. Slinging the Schmeisser back over his shoulder, he climbed to the top of one of the railcars. Folding out the flexible antennae, Paul hit the panic key which transmitted an encrypted message with his location while he scanned behind him with the binoculars.

Back at the Communications Center in Retreat 2, Master Sergeant Lancon spotted the alarm. He flipped several switches as he plugged his own headset into the console. "Rabbit, this is the Hooch, SITREP, over."

"Hooch, this is Rabbit. Engaged by hostiles, need assistance and evac, over."

Lancon studied the display which showed Rubenstein's location with a blinking red light. He flipped a switch and the display changed to a real time video display from a satellite feed. "Roger, Rabbit... I have your location... you have bogies approaching on foot, estimating arrival in ten to fifteen minutes. Suggest you go to ground, I'm sending the cavalry, over."

"Roger, Hooch. Rabbit, out." Rubenstein climbed back down and stowed the comm set. He was trapped. But, he had some protection from the two railcars and he had the Harley plugging one end of the box he had formed. He crawled under one of the rail cars and laid the comm set alongside of a rail. He unsnapped the safety strap on his tanker-style shoulder rig supporting the Browning Hi-Power and laid the extra Schmeisser magazines on the ground next to him before putting an earplug in each ear. Firing the Schmeisser and the Browning in the relatively close quarters under the railcar would kill his hearing.

He waited, it would not be long.

Chapter Sixty-Seven

It had been almost thirty minutes by Rubenstein's watch, he wondered if he had lost his pursuers... Then he saw a man on foot, then another. As they got closer, Paul could tell they were carrying military-style automatic rifles. They had the advantage of range over his Schmeisser and Browning.

While they have the advantage of range and weaponry, their tactics leave much to be desired, Paul decided. They were not patrolling, they were walking. *No weapon discipline*, he noticed. *Two have their rifles lying across their shoulders.*

As they drew closer, Paul laid the Schmeisser aside and drew his Hi-Power. While the Schmeisser had great firepower, the Browning was better suited to accuracy. He drew a bead on the closest man, at what he guessed was about seventy-five yards; Paul fired.

Even though he missed the man, the shot was successful in that it reminded his pursuers that the game was not over yet. His pursuers dispersed and tried to figure out where the shot had come from. Rubenstein glanced at his watch, *Come on Cavalry... come on!*

The bad guys broke cover and began advancing. Paul recognized the advance was a poor attempt at the fire and movement technique known as leapfrogging. In leapfrogging, one team suppresses the enemy while the other moves either toward the enemy or to a more favorable position. In this case, a couple of people were firing ineffective shots in a variety of directions without knowing where Paul actually was, while others ran helter-skelter trying to find him.

Paul drew another bead on an approaching hunter and squeezed. This time a 115 grain slug slammed into the man's mid-section throwing him backwards. He screamed. He kept screaming until Paul sent a mercy slug into his braincase. The echoes around the rail yard continued to confuse his trackers. It was like he was a ghost.

One of them stood and either purposefully or accidentally began walking straight toward Paul's hiding place, with what appeared to be an ancient selective switched M-14 .308 battle rifle. Paul holstered the Browning and picked up the Schmeisser. With the long thirty-two round magazine, the Schmeisser is not the best weapon when firing from a prone position, but it can be done.

Paul did not believe the approaching hunter knew where he was but he kept getting closer and, in a few more feet, he was sure the man would spot him. At less than twenty feet, Paul sent a short burst of three rounds into the man's chest. The man flew backwards, his M-14 landed close to Paul's position. It appeared there was a full magazine in the weapon and a makeshift ammo pouch attached to the rear stock, containing another magazine.

Paul weighed his choices. If he moved... he would be spotted and killed in a fusillade of bullets. If he did not try for the M-14, he remained totally out gunned. Suddenly, he heard precisely targeted rounds being fired... fired at his pursuers.

He scanned the area but could not see the shooters; then he heard the sounds of engine noise approaching. He slid out from under the railcar, crab-walked quickly to the M-14 and then crawled back under the railcar. He checked the chamber and sent a .308 round down range at a man that exposed his head. At a little over two hundred yards, the 7.62x51mm NATO slug entered the man's face just below his nose. It tore through his front teeth, through the back of the mouth and blasted tissue and bone out the back of his neck as it severed the spinal column.

Rounds began to ping out the railcar wheel between which Paul was hiding. The metal sides of the cars themselves could not withstand the impact of the .308 and 5.56 rounds his attackers fired at Paul. He was glad he had not counted on the steel of the railcar as a hiding place.

He spotted movement off to the left, a shooter. But this shooter was not aiming at Paul and he was using a hunting rifle, a bolt action. Paul watched. Four rounds fired, four of his attackers downed… Paul had help.

Paul and his unknown helper continued to fire into his attackers. Paul's first magazine was empty and as he changed magazines; he watched as the unknown shooter dispatched three more bad guys.

Paul was halfway through his second twenty-five round magazine when the shooting stopped. After a couple of moments of silence, Paul crawled slowly from beneath the railcar. Standing he saw his ally waving and waved back. That's when a man landed on Paul's back knocking him to the ground and sending his wire framed glasses spinning in the dirt.

The impact sent Paul rolling but before he could catch his breath the man was on him again. A heavy fist slammed into the side of Paul's face spinning him around. Paul was stunned and watched helplessly as the bigger man removed the Browning from the shoulder holster. Paul pulled the Marine Ka-Bar from the sheath on his belt and shoved upward. Arguably the most famous fixed blade knife in the world, the Ka-Bar boasted a seven-inch blade with a clip point.

That clip point entered the attacker's left leg just to the inside of the thigh and continued on upward until it was stopped by the hip joint. The man bellowed as blood began spurting from the severed femoral artery. The Browning Hi-Power dropped to the ground and the man collapsed. Paul jerked hard on the stack-leather, washer handle; the point of the blade was stuck in the hip joint.

The man screamed once and passed out from the blood loss and pain. Even if Paul had wanted to save the man, there was little that could have been done. Rourke had told him the adult human heart pumps several liters of blood per minute and the average human male only has about four or five liters of blood.

Moments later the man was dead. Paul picked up the Hi-Power. People were running toward him, Paul recognized Lane Alexander carrying a rifle and his son Noah leading two horses behind his father. Suddenly there was a blinding green flash and everything stopped.

Chapter Sixty-Eight

Master Sergeant Lancon had dispatched an Egg and a squad of Wes Sanderson's Marines to rescue Paul. A second Egg with the other half of that squad had maintained overwatch while the rescue squad had brought Paul, Lane and Noah Alexander on board and moved the bodies of those that had attacked Paul inside one of the railcars and retrieved their weapons.

That Egg was returned to Retreat 2.

Alexander's horses were too large to fit through the hatch of The Egg. Two of Sanderson's Marines had agreed to ride them back to Retreat 2 and the second Egg followed providing cover in case of a second follow up attack.

Paul, Lane, and Noah regained consciousness aboard The Egg before it landed. Chief Wes Sanderson wanted to interview them. "How did you end up at the attack, Mr. Alexander... you and Noah that is?"

"I saw that several of our citizens had left the Underground before Mr. Rubenstein," Lane Alexander explained. Turning toward Paul, he continued, "I wasn't sure why but I figured it wouldn't hurt if I followed you. I wish I could have warned you earlier but our Mayor White wouldn't leave your side."

"So, you think White was involved in this?" Paul asked.

Alexander shook his head. "I don't know... I don't want to think so, but... let's just say I can't exclude the possibility. Since our initial contact with your people, things at the Underground have been... different, Mr. Rubenstein."

"Different, how?"

"I don't know that I can explain it. There have been a lot of meetings, closed meetings between the Mayor and several groups of citizens.

What I can tell you is the people that attacked you have been participants in several of those meetings."

Paul frowned. "Why would they attack me; why didn't White simply capture me while I was in the Underground with your people?"

Alexander shook his head. "I don't know. Maybe they did not want the rest of our citizens to be aware of your capture... or your death."

Paul frowned. "Yes, that is a valid point, since the attack was not particularly well coordinated, even I can't say whether it was a snatch and grab or an assassination attempt. What now?"

Noah spoke up for the first time, "Mr. Rubenstein, I don't think my dad and I should go back to the Underground. At least, not yet... not until we find out more about what is going on."

Lane Alexander nodded. "I agree with my son. I fear us returning could place us in jeopardy and in turn jeopardize the situation between our two peoples. I've known Mayor White all of my life. He has been a good mayor but since we learned of your existence... he simply has not been the same."

"When exactly did you learn of our existence?" Paul asked.

"Some time ago, actually," Alexander said.

Sanderson sat up straight. "So, when Hiram Wesson and his son came here... you are saying it was not an accident. They didn't just stumble onto us?"

Alexander shook his head. "Tell them, Noah."

Noah cleared his throat, "Two days before Billy Wesson shot your men he told me that he and his father were going to do something 'special' for Mayor White. Mr. Rubenstein, I swear I did not know they were going to hurt anybody."

"But why did Billy do it, Noah?" Paul asked.

"I don't think he did Mr. Rubenstein." Noah said, his voice cracking a little, "I've known Billy all of my life, we were best friends. I don't think he shot anyone."

"But his own father said he did…"

Alexander shook his head. "Not his own father… his stepfather. Hiram Wesson was Billy's stepfather and he was a mean, nasty bully. I think Hiram shot those two men and since Billy had been killed by return fire from your soldiers… why not blame a dead kid and save himself?"

*****

James White, Mayor of the Underground was pacing; there still was no word from those he had sent to capture Paul Rubenstein. He mumbled to himself as he paced, "Damn Rubenstein and his people. Why did they have to come now? Why did they have to come at all?"

White realized he was addicted. Strange that until these outsiders came into his world he would have never guessed he was afflicted. His sickness was greed, greed or avarice, the inordinate or insatiable longing for material gain. White knew that in his personal case, it was not about food or money or even sex. It was totally about status and power. He suffered from the inordinate desire to acquire or possess more status and power.

Chapter Sixty-Nine

Chief Sanderson terminated the meeting and had Lane Alexander and his son Noah, placed in protective custody. "Mr. Alexander… I hope you understand. It is my responsibility to maintain security for Retreat 2 and frankly… right now, I'm just not sure about you and your son. Until I am, you will be treated fairly and generously and as a guest and not a prisoner. However, I hope you understand you will be watched and watched closely."

Alexander nodded. "I understand and I think you are being both appropriate and generous under the circumstances. Frankly, Chief Sanderson, I don't believe that you have any other choice. Personally, I am more comfortable with being in 'custody' with your people than in being free with my own.

"I think in short order, you will learn my son and I are not a threat to you and your people. I have lived with my own people all of my life and I'm no longer sure my son and I are protected. I accept your 'invitation,' Sir."

*****

Sanderson sat back down after Alexander and his son left. He shook his head. "Paul, I'm confused. This Lane Alexander is not like anyone I've ever met before. You can tell he's smart, but he doesn't make a show of it. You watched him methodically shoot down some of his own people to protect you… an outsider. And now, he thanks me for my 'invitation' to have him and his son placed in protective custody until I'm comfortable he is not a threat…"

Paul smiled. "I think you have a unique individual here. Confident but not braggadocios, competent but also somewhat restrained, well rounded without making a big deal about it. I like the guy."

Sanderson smiled. "Of course you do, he saved your butt out there at the rail cars."

Chapter Seventy

Dr. David Blackman, Chief of Psychological Research at Mid-Wake, and Dr. Henry Drake, Chief of Medicine at Tripler, sat in Blackman's office at Mid-Wake. Drake said, "I just don't understand the medical aspects of this case. She is a seasoned combat veteran."

"Henry, you are mixing apples and oranges. She is a seasoned combat, but aerial combat veteran. Combat pilots kill planes not people."

"But the planes are piloted by people."

"Of course they are and as a result, those people die. But it is different from say an infantry soldier that sees the person they are going to kill as another human being. Studies all the way back to 1921 when the Italian infantry officer Giulio Douhet became the world's first air power theoretician to have struggled with the mental aspects of war and conflict and death and mental stability.

"Studies have shown the dynamics of 'becoming' a psychological casualty are complex," Blackman said. "Even the medical side of treatment can vary based on the 'type' of psychological casualty. For example, PTSD or Post Traumatic Stress Disorder, develops in people who have experienced a shocking, scary, or dangerous event. But it is more of a complex issue than originally thought.

"There is more involved than just the recognized 'fight-or-flight' response that is a typical reaction meant to protect a person from harm. Direct participants and indirect participants in warfare react differently. Anger, fear, loss, and violence have some degree of effect on everyone, but NOT THE SAME DEGREE of effect. It is grossly unfair for people who have not killed to try and understand the psychological aspects of killing. One theorist said it is like a virgin trying to study sex.

"You can get the mechanics right but not understand the intensity or intimacy created by the act. Furthermore, sex and killing are two of the most intense and intimate things humans do. The third is dying and I postulate that our patient's biggest issue is not how many she has killed but how much the death of those people now coupled with the death of her child and the possibility of death for her husband and now the restructuring of her entire life and future have affected her."

Dr. Drake nodded. "I agree and all of that has a tremendous impact on how I can treat her medically. I can heal her body, David..."

"I know Henry... but I'm not sure I can heal her mind... or her soul."

Chapter Seventy-One

Colonel Mikhail Sergeyevich found himself torn; torn emotionally between his duty and his lust. Between the path his life had been set on and the path of pleasure that Andrea van Arnstein's body had shown him. On one hand, the pragmatic soldier he was, scoffed at the ludicrous notion that a simple female should have the ability to pull him away from his mission.

However, Andrea van Arnstein was NOT a simple female and, in fairness to Colonel Sergeyevich, it should be acknowledged that one of his own KGB's favorite methods of recruiting traitors and spies was simply called "the honey pot." In the terminology of espionage, the "honey pot" and "honey trap" were terms for recruitment involving sexual seduction. And in fairness, the trap worked equally well when the target was a woman.

Intellectually, Sergeyevich understood what was happening but emotionally was incapable or unwilling to stop it. It seems that the way to a man's heart did not just lie with his stomach. *But I am a Colonel in the KGB*, Mikhail thought. *After all, I am actually the one using her for my own pleasure. She is simply an upper crust tart with a flair for kinky sex, therein lays her weakness... not mine.* Her hands closed on him again and he struggled against the restraints and the gag in his mouth, in his mind he shouted, *I am in control.* In his passion he silently whimpered, *I am lost.*

"Truly, tell me what you want, Mikhail," she whispered as she removed his gag.

"You and everything about you," he answered.

"Tell me about your mission, everything about your mission and I will give myself to you... totally," she whispered as she flipped the hidden switch for the recorder.

And he told her about his mission, everything about his mission.

Chapter Seventy-Two

Roderick van Arnstein listened with disgust to the tape recording, his sister… his very own sister… how could she? He looked over at her, his eyes hard. If she read his face, she deemed not to mention it.

"Dear brother, our new world order is about to spring forth full grown and vital. The dramatic change in world politics and the balance of power our family has sought for so long… it is here. Our concept of global governance will not simply be a cluster of systems to manage governments but the capacity to problem solve all nations… all nations across the globe with one direction and set of specific goals that we shall enunciate.

"From Woodrow Wilson's Fourteen Points through the League of Nations and then the United Nations and so many other attempts to unify this entire planet for centuries… we arrive at this great junction. Finally, after generations upon generations have sought an elusive peace… while wars burned in every corner of the globe and in the hearts of mankind himself. We stand on the verge of a new world about to be born… a world quite different from the one we've known."

"Yes, dear sister, I agree… however, I disagree with your methods. I disagree with how you gather your information." Roderick looked at his sister, she was incredible, beautiful, and intelligent but flawed. She laughed and he slapped her hard across the mouth.

His temper flared. "I have told you repeatedly that WE, you and I, have a responsibility to the cause, to this cause, to OUR cause. If we do not sanctify it with our actions and our behavior, who will? We must become more than we have ever been, dear sister. We, our actions, our every action must be strong enough to serve as our legacy long after you and I are dead and gone.

"We must be strong enough to create and sustain a dynasty that will last till the end of time. THAT is what you and I have been bred for, that is what we have been created to do. But you conduct yourself like a little trollop who provides sexual favors to people she might not even know and demands no money for her services. You have been bred to rule the world beside me, but you display the loose morals of someone who lacks confidence in her own worth. How is this possible?"

Chapter Seventy-Three

Command Sergeant Major Harvey Bishop, Retired, turned toward General Sullivan and asked, "How... how could this happen? What went wrong? How did the world get so screwed up?

Sullivan poured another two fingers of whiskey in his glass and proffered the bottle to Bishop and growled, "For Pete's sake Harvey, don't go back to that 'single cause' nonsense, you know it is crap. We as humans tend toward causal oversimplification, causal reductionism, and reduction fallacy.

"After a tragedy, everyone asks, "What caused this?" The reality is not one thing usually causes anything. Usually, there are a bunch of 'things' that interrelate to cause something. What causes a school shooting or a run on a bank or a war or an illness? The truth is a lot of things go together to make up the circumstance that creates each of these situations and a lot more to boot."

Harvey took the bottle and poured libation for himself. "I know all of that General, what I want to know is this. How... how could this happen? What went wrong?"

Sullivan raised his glass in a toast to his oldest and only true friend, "People. That's what went wrong and is the reason this could happen. It happened because of people, no more complicated or simplified than that. We are after all a rather stupid and belligerent species you know."

Bishop returned the toast gesture and said, "So nothing could have stopped this? Is that what you're saying?"

Sullivan shook his head. "Nope Harvey, not at all. In fact, the very thing that created this mess is the very thing that could have stopped it. People created it and people could have stopped it. But no one did."

"Did we just not see it?"

Sullivan frowned. "That's what bothers me, Harvey. A few of us did. You and I saw it coming; the Rourkes sure saw it coming. I'm sure some others did also but it wasn't enough to stop it from happening. It's been that way throughout human history. For a special few the signs are obvious but for the vast majority of folks, the signs are invisible or not relevant to their own individual lives. But then there is the other side of the equation, Harvey."

"What is the other side of the equation? What does it look like?"

Sullivan looked down in his glass and swirled the dark whiskey around, then quickly brought the glass up to his lips and slugged it down. "The other side of the equation, Sergeant Major, is evil. Often seductive and lovely, sometimes it is ugly and powerful. What does it look like? Like Hitler and Eugenics and the New World Order, like Brown Shirts and black robes, like cowboys and Indians... evil most often looks like what a very few people want to impose on a whole bunch of people and ALWAYS for the best reasons and intentions."

Bishop chugged his drink and sat the glass down on the coffee table. "Always, General?"

Sullivan stood up and said, "Always, Harvey, or at least every time I have ever seen it happen."

"So, what do we do about it this time, General?

Sullivan looked at Bishop and smiled as his placed his hand on Bishop's shoulder, "Why, Harvey Bishop... you old softy. We fight it like hell. We kick evil's butt all the way out the door. We kill every SOB that is on evil's side. We tear down everything that evil builds. We cut the head off of evil and then sprinkle salt on the stump so it won't grow back."

"And that will stop evil, General. Is that what you're telling me?"

"For a while, Harvey... for a while."

Chapter Seventy-Four

President Greene opened the first News Coordination Summit, "Ladies and Gentlemen... the time has come for responsible journalism and common sense actions to join forces. The days of rabblerousing for the sake of ratings and corporate positioning have passed.

"You, the members of the Fourth Estate, have a responsibility TO the public not FOR the public. How can you imagine that true progress can be gained by divisive articles and stories that allow the multitude to wander aimlessly through conflict after conflict without direction?

"How can you expect the common man to assimilate the masses of relevant information and move appropriately through this crisis on their own?"

Bill Nolan from DOT, Dead on Target Television, raised his hand. "Mr. President, in the Bill of Rights, the First Amendment to the Constitution says, and I quote, 'Congress shall make no law respecting an establishment of religion, or prohibiting the free exercise thereof; or abridging the freedom of speech, or of the press; or the right of the people peaceably to assemble, and to petition the Government for redress of grievances.'"

Greene dabbed his lip with his handkerchief. "You are correct, Bill. As usual, you are 'dead on target.'" The audience laughed on the play on words.

Nolan smiled. "Mr. President, there are rumors circulating that the reason for this News Coordination Summit is to circumvent the First Amendment."

"Bill, that rumor is another lie being spread by the ongoing conspiracy that assails my administration. The First Amendment is one of the cornerstones this country was founded on. But, there are some points that

I believe are relevant, not least of which is the fact that the first ten amendments, collectively known as the Bill of Rights, were ratified December 15… 1791. 1791 Bill… how can we be tied to and expected to legislate by virtue of a document that was written over 850 years in the past?

"It was written before the Night of the War that almost destroyed not only this country but the entire world. A world that when that document was ratified had no concept of alien life forms and thought Atlantis was merely a story thought up by an ancient Greek named Homer."

Agnes Briggs from Honolulu's largest newspaper, the World Associated Press, raised her hand. "Mr. President…"

Greene frowned then recovered his pleasant demeanor. "Yes Agnes, what is it?"

"Plato."

"Plato?"

Agnes smiled. "Yes, Mr. President… it was Plato that wrote about Atlantis. Homer did the Iliad and the Odyssey."

Greene continued to smile, except with his eyes. *Now,* he thought. *This is exactly the kind of opening I was waiting on.* "Agnes, this… clarification that you just made is the reason for this Summit. Thank you for bringing us to the denouement."

"Denouement, Sir?" Agnes asked with a smile.

"Yes Agnes, the denouement… the final part of a play, movie, or narrative in which the strands of the plot are drawn together and matters are explained or resolved." Greene reached into his inside jacket pocket and removed a set of folded notes and opened them. "Ladies and Gentlemen, I have a full day of very important business today, serious business that requires my personal attention. I and our country have no more time to lose to minor obstructionists and meaningless banter. Ergo, there will be no further questions from the floor.

"Instead, my staff will make available to you and your news agencies the following documents and instructions. These instructions are being implemented immediately for the safety and security of our citizens. Compliance with each of these instructions is required, any media company failing to comply will be found guilty of sedition. To be clear, sedition is defined as 'overt conduct, such as speech and organization that tends toward insurrection against the established order and or incitement of discontent towards, or resistance against established authority, specifically the government of the United States.'"

Bill Nolan stood. "Mr. President, without even hearing what these instructions are, I challenge your authority to make these changes... before you read these instructions I must remind you that the Bill of Rights specifically says..."

President of the United States, Phillip Greene, slammed his hand down on the podium. "Mr. Nolan... As you are aware, Mr. Nolan, there are three branches to the Federal Government; equal but separate. They are the judicial branch which includes the Supreme Court with nine Justices. They are special judges who interpret laws according to the Constitution. These justices only hear cases that pertain to issues related to the Constitution. They are the highest court in our country. The federal judicial system also has lower courts located in each state to hear cases involving federal issues.

"The next is the Legislative branch, collectively known as Congress. Congress makes our laws. Congress is divided into two parts. One part is called the Senate and the other is the House of Representatives.

"Then there is the Executive branch or, the President of the United States, who administers the Executive Branch of our government. The President enforces the laws that the Legislative Branch, Congress, makes. I am not creating laws; I am protecting our citizens and our country from traitors.

"Ladies and Gentlemen, while there have been no further attacks for the past weeks… we are at war. While I have attempted to move cautiously and gently, by virtue of my war powers as President, the Constitution promised the holder of this position authority that he might use the military, absent a Congressional declaration of war… and the scope of such power. I am enacting an executive order which has the same power as federal law.

"I assure you these instructions are perfectly legal under Article II of the Constitution which gives specific emergency powers to the president. I have the power to sign or veto legislation. I serve notice that any legislative attempt by Congress to impede or disregard these instructions will not pass. I command the armed forces and have already sent orders to all commanders that any attempt by any organization or individual to subvert these instructions must be stopped and stopped with force if necessary.

"I have asked for and received written opinions of my Cabinet and they are in one hundred percent support of these instructions. Last night I did convene an emergency session of Congress which failed to support these measures. As a result until further notice, Congress, by virtue of my emergency powers, is adjourned.

"Lastly, my abilities to grant reprieves and pardons and receive ambassadors are not affected by these instructions. Mr. Nolan, you have won the lottery and a place in history; congratulations."

"Mr. President…"

"Bill, you are the first to challenge these instructions. I knew there would be someone but did not know it would be you. You and I are about to step into history together. You, as the deluded fool who tried to hold onto an outdated concept known as the First Amendment; and me, the farsighted President that saved his country and possibly the world from suffering and slavery."

Greene turned to his head of security, pointed at Bill Nolan and said, "Arrest that man for sedition."

Chapter Seventy-Five

"John, I see you carry several knives. I am particularly interested in the one on your belt."

Rourke unsnapped the sheath and pulled the Fighting Bowie out, rolled it between his fingers and handed the knife butt first. "Grigori, this knife was made for me before the Night of the War. I had a friend named Hank Frost; Hank worked a lot as a mercenary and he knew two knife makers: Ed Martin and his son Newton, Newt for short. I had been working on two knife designs and if there was anything the one-eyed mercenary knew about, it was knives. Frost told me to get with the Martins on my designs.

"Newt was home on leave from the Navy, he was a submariner. His father Ed and his uncle Hank Martin had been 'playing' at knife making for years. Playing meant they made good quality using knives '…but we're still playing with our own designs,' Newt told me.

"Anyway I showed them the designs and to quote a guy named Jim Bowie from an old movie. I said, 'I've seen guns fail. I've seen swords fail. I want something that won't fail,' and I want two of them. One, a Bowie fighter and the other, a spear point dive knife, small enough to carry concealed if necessary but big enough and strong enough to hang my life on if need be.

"This Fighting Bowie is out of quarter inch stock with integral guards top and bottom. As you can see, it has some 'very aggressive' serrations and a skull crusher at the end of the handle with a thong hole. Lastly, the handle is the type that you can fight with the blade upright or a reverse grip."

"Have you actually fought with this knife?"

"Oh, yes. I seem to keep running into people that don't like me. With the sheath, I can carry the Bowie conventionally on my belt or mounted horizontally in the back or on the side for cross draw. Both carry this emblem; it is my initials."

"If you don't mind me asking, how long did it take them to make a knife like this?"

Rourke smiled. "They wanted a month to complete both knives but I only had a little over two weeks, I was finishing up one job and about to start another. Ed asked Newt, 'Whatcha think, son?' Newt rubbed his face and said, 'It will be tight but I think we can do it.' Ed said, 'Alright, if you don't mind us putting our mark on the back side of the blade…this knife might be famous one day.' I used them one time and then three months later the end of my world started… the Night of the War. I had them both stored in my original Retreat until last year."

Grigori smiled. "I prefer a longer blade myself."

"I carried a longer blade myself for a long time. It was the Crain LSX, really the size of a small sword," Rourke said.

Grigori's smile broadened. "I like the full size one best."

Rourke tilted his head to one side. "I take it you fence? Foil, epee or saber?"

"All three but I am fastest with the foil and strongest with the epee. I am still working to master the saber. Would you join me for a practice match?"

"I'm afraid I'm a knife fighter, not a sword fighter," Rourke said, smiling.

"It is a sport for gentlemen; it possesses the essence of discipline and technique. Come, I will show you."

*****

Grigori Ragulin came out of the dressing room dressed in white and carrying a matched set of fencing foils. Giving one to Rourke he said, "These have the French grip, it looks uncomfortable but once you see how it sits in your hand... well, try it. It is slightly curved and offers flexibility as you may choose to either hold the grip near the pommel to allow for longer reach while decreasing the potency of parries and beats, or closer to the guard for more force and a shorter reach. In competitive fencing, only epee fencers use French grip. In actuality, there are many different types of French grip and each epee fencer eventually ends up using a single type which better fits their style of fencing.

He showed Rourke how to hold the handle. "Oh, yes," Rourke said. "I see what you mean."

Ragulin spent about fifteen minutes going over the basics with Rourke. Everything from the foible, the flexible tip section of the blade, to how to stand and how to hold the arms. Finally, he said, "Shall we begin?"

Ragulin said, "I am wearing a mask because you are unskilled. For this class, you need not worry about it; I am skilled enough not to injure you, my friend."

Rourke smiled. "Okay... my friend let us begin. But remember I take injury very seriously."

Grigori laughed, pulled on his mask with its fabric neck guard and said, "En garde." When Rourke pulled on his mask and assumed the position, beneath the Russian's face mask, the smile on Grigori's face disappeared.

Click, click, click, advance, retreat, lunge, parry, click, click, click.

Rourke began to understand what Ragulin had meant about discipline and technique. Whereas blocking and parrying with a knife often required strength, with the foil it was all about speed and deflection.

Click, click, click, advance, retreat, lunge, parry, click, click, click.

Forward and backward along the mat, the two moved with grace, admittedly more so the Russian than Rourke. Click, click, click, advance, retreat, lunge, parry, click, click, click. Grigori called a halt. "John, you are a quick study... I'm pleased."

"Thank you... but I have to tell you... this feels stupid. This isn't fighting to me."

Grigori smiled. "Of course not... that's because it is not fighting... it is fencing. The roots came from sword fighting in the Middle Ages but now it is simply a sport. Who cares about three feet of steel anymore when with a rifle you can kill at several hundred meters? Here, technique is everything and improvement is measured not by how many opponents you defeat but how many techniques you can master."

The "class" lasted an hour and at the end, Rourke was surprised to find himself winded while Ragulin was not.

Chapter Seventy-Six

"There shall be NO censorship." Paul Rubenstein flipped off the news broadcasts. "That is the way it starts, 'There shall be NO censorship. However, we must develop some common sense measures that allow for the safety and security of our citizens.' In fact, that is the way it always starts."

Noah Alexander spoke up, "But these are just common sense measures to protect our citizens."

Michael Rourke smiled. "The problem with common sense approaches is there is seldom any common sense applied to the approaches."

Noah's father, Lane, said, "But even the Christians agreed to the public decency provisions. Private publications have exploded thanks to technology. Even the common household can actually publish a book now and some of them are terrible. Of course, distribution is still a problem thank goodness, but occasionally some really bad works make their way into the mainstream of society."

Paul Rubenstein said, "I have tracked those cases over the past weeks, over a hundred to date and no one who really examined those cases was ever able to say exactly how they did it but when cases were brought against specific individuals, it was obvious by the media coverage they were guilty and guilty as sin. Now, throughout the world theaters, cinemas, cabarets, and private clubs are subject to state licensing. Police have direct control over these venues.

"The entertainment business has to make sure all of their films respect the standards established by the government. 'We must remain loyal to our country in this time of stress and crisis. Compliance during times of stress and crisis work toward the common good.' Resources could be properly marshaled to return power and services to full operational stability quicker.

"From time to time, something less than seditious but more than 'troubling' might be printed, labeled as 'inappropriate materials.' These resulted in punitive fines or operational suspensions that could last days or weeks. Another point of interest dealt with programming for preschool through adolescent citizens. Removal of all rap music was met with approval by older citizens but simply drove the music underground.

"Under the guidance of the Citizens for Responsible Media, all things dealing with social, religious, ethical, or world-view-related topics were scrutinized. 'Of course, pornography and other indecent content should finally be eliminated from our society,' the Reverend William Eckhart pronounced from the pulpit. Under the guidance of the Citizens for Responsible Media and the second and third News Coordination Summits, the censorship that is not supposed to be has only gotten worse."

Michael sat frowning. "Paul, how long has it been since the initial attack by the Russians and the KI?"

"Not quite three months now. Why?"

Rourke stood. "Three months... three months and outside of the initial surrenders of the governments of the world there have been no formal statements from the victors of those attacks. Back in 1933, after the Nazis rose to power, there were book burnings. One-third of all of the library books in Germany went up in smoke to shouts of 'No to decadence and moral corruption!' All to illustrate government control and align public opinion with party ideology. We know there was Neo-Nazi involvement before the attacks. Why have they not surfaced after the attacks? Why haven't the Russians been making demands, why haven't they landed troops? Where are the occupying forces from the KI Empire, why haven't they landed? There has been no official contact from either."

"No official contact that we know of…" Rubenstein said. "Michael, what do you have to say about that?"

Michael shook his head. "Has there been contact, official or not… no! We, or rather at least I, would know about it. That is one of the most important parts of Operation Phoenix—information management. Accurate real-time information no one knows we have access to."

"Michael, have your people learned anything more about those folks that "Beaux" Delys, Otto and Tuviah Friedman discovered in France?"

Michael shook his head. "Nothing. Following the assassinations of Delys and Friedman, there has been nothing. Now that Otto is escorting the children back to Camp Zero for the next phases of their training, we need another plan and another operative to work that plan."

Paul nodded. "Any idea who?"

Chapter Seventy-Seven

Alexander Corti, head of the Intelligence Committee, and Demetrius Conte, head of the Continuity Committee, stood next to a large frame that contained a huge wall map. It almost covered one entire side of the Grand Hall. It had been assembled during the night for today's meeting; it was too large to enter either of the ten feet tall double oak doors on either side of the huge fireplace that warmed the forty-five by sixty-five feet Grand Hall.

Today the six massive chandeliers had been removed and modern electric lighting filled the chamber. The smell of fresh furniture polish filled the hall and the large plain rectangular table's surface shined. Around the table sat forty-eight heavy wood and leather chairs. At the end of the table, nearest the lit fireplace, set a larger, forty-ninth chair. In front of each chair, sitting almost anachronism to this dark, heavy and solemn atmosphere was an open laptop computer, its screen illuminated and ready for use.

There came a soft, barely audible gong sound and the double oak doors on either side of the lighted fireplace opened. Andrea von Arnstein entered from the left door and began walking forward; others followed her. Another line of walkers began from the left door, but the first person was even with the person directly behind the attractive older woman. In slow, measured steps the two lines moved down opposite sides of the long table. She stood at the end of the table while the others stood in front of their assigned places. A second, barely audible gong sounded and a tall, slender man entered from the right door; Roderick von Arnstein.

He walked to his position at the head of the great table; the quorum was complete. At his direction everyone took their seats, everyone except Alexander Corti, head of the Intelligence Committee, and Demetrius Conte, head of the Continuity Committee; they continued to stand at attention next to the huge map.

Roderick picked up the small engraved bell made from the very best German silver over 700 years old; giving a flick of his wrist, it tingled. The doors on either side of the fireplace opened again. From the left, down came the Russian Colonel, Mikhail Sergeyevich, survivor of Karamatsov's KGB Elite Corps.

Pathetic peacock, Roderick thought to himself.

From the right door came the KI Empire representative. He was taller than Roderick by almost a foot and Roderick stood over six feet. The KI's complexion was a golden hue, almost like burnished bronze, an impression heightened by his uniform, a form fitted, golden jumpsuit.

Walking on opposite sides of the long table they met at the end and turned to face the others.

Roderick stood and addressed his congregants first, "Lokhagos is the KI word for Captain." He addressed the KI, "Lokhagos, I am afraid you are out of uniform."

The KI Captain was taken back and quickly checked the few accouterments on his uniform. "I am sorry but you are mistaken, Sir. My uniform is, as always, correct."

Roderick moved from the head of the table and walked to the KI. "Correct for a Captain of the KI, to be sure. However, it is not correct for a Tagmatarkhis, a Battalion Leader." Roderick presented a rank insignia and speaking in perfect KI said, "Tagmatarkhis, you have done your job well and now are rewarded with a promotion."

The Tagmatarkhis looked surprised as Roderick affixed the insignia. It was old beyond belief, ancient and weathered... but it was for a KI Battalion Leader... a Tagmatarkhis. "How is it you speak the KI language? I have been told it is unknown to humans."

Roderick smiled and continued on in KI, "To humans yes, but not to your descendants. Tagmatarkhis, centuries ago when the Great War came and the KI left... not all of your people were able to leave Earth. Many were stranded here for all time. Most survived as best they could and became legends and gods to the humans, but a small select group was able to find refuge in a KI outpost that survived the turmoil and devastation that racked the planet.

"This outpost was on the continent at what is now Earth's South Pole. The very continent the KI Armada chose to establish orbit over when you returned. Over the millennia, they died but not before establishing a legacy. They interbred with humans but never lost their identity as KI, nor their science, nor... as you see, our language. For all of my ancestors... for all of the fathers and mothers and brothers and sisters that did not live to see your return... welcome. Welcome, Home."

The Tagmatarkhis stood, staring before finally speaking, "It was known that many failed to join the fleet in time. Many of our families lost loved ones when that final battle took place. Their names were entered on our scrolls in the Hall of Heroes. We will celebrate together, both our return to the home planet and your return to the parents of your parents a thousand times over. Within your bodies is the indelible mark of the KI. Even after all of this time, we should be able to identify your family or families if they still exist."

Chapter Seventy-Eight

Dr. David Blackman, Chief of Psychological Research at Mid-Wake, was exhausted. In addition to a full schedule of patients experiencing extreme anxiety and psychopathy, there were the meetings. Governmental representatives were monitoring Blackman's research with a fine-toothed comb and Blackman was convinced the monitoring had nefarious tendencies.

Rather than looking for positive therapeutic processes, the monitoring seemed to be going in the other direction; looking for the bad rather than the good. Blackman turned; Dr. Henry Drake, Chief of Medicine at Tripler, had knocked on his door. "Henry, I thought you had left to go back to Hawaii. Come on in."

Drake entered the office, turned and leaned out into the hallway and scanned in both directions before closing the door. "David, we need to talk. I just left a very interesting meeting with one of the medical bureaucrats. I have some concerns and I want to bounce them off of you."

"Go ahead." Blackman poured two cups of coffee and sat one in front of Drake. "What is going on?"

Drake sipped his coffee. "Not anything in my arena, except maybe tangentially. But I'm pretty convinced it is absolutely in your expertise. I think these bureaucrats are looking to find a way to locate or create people whose illness make them particularly susceptible to suggestion or... or even mind control. I know it is possible but is it practical?"

Blackman thought for a moment and said, "Sure it is. The founder of behaviorism, John Watson, once postulated that if you gave him a dozen healthy infants, well-formed, and his own specified world to bring them up in, he would guarantee to be able to take anyone at random and train him to become any type of specialist Watson might need. Take that one step further and not only is it possible to mold someone into a psychopath… it is probable.

"All you would need is an environment that is characterized by a lack of empathy and is full of selfishness and deceitfulness. Although certain genes may predispose people toward psychopathy, their environment seems to provide the ultimate catalyst. So, whether or not a person possesses the particular genes associated with this malady, when someone is brought up in an abusive or neglectful household, they will be at a higher risk of exhibiting the traits associated with this disorder. It is not guaranteed but it is a pretty good bet."

"So, you are saying if you take bullies, and tell them it is okay to be bullies and take the disenfranchised and tell them it is okay to persecute their tormentors… they will probably do it?"

"Yep. We see it all the time with opposing political groups. Once they start disrupting the meetings of their opponents, it is usually a downhill slide to intimating minorities, fighting, looting, and rioting.

"Henry, right now our whole world culture is ripe for this kind of madness, especially after the attacks and the capitulation of the governments. I think the only reason things have not really exploded is no one has stepped in to take over; it is really brilliant if you think about it. Let the peasants stew in their own juices, let their imaginations fill them with fear and when you do finally step into the limelight, if you are halfway reasonable or at least not as bad as their imagination… you have control and willing followers.

"We're at the point where it is no longer a question of societal survivalism, it is overcoming the present. When large-scale change takes place in the contemporary world, a system-wide shock surges through the population. Not only is there the physical dynamics of death and destruction to deal with, but there is also the reality that there no longer is a 'normal.'

"Nothing is the same anymore and nothing ever will be the same again. Ergo, the societal body begins to either evolve or devolve to a new normal. Most if not all of the beliefs and institutions that once anchored international and domestic affairs have grown weak or have died.

"Where there has been physical destruction there have also been political tidal waves that drowned normality wherever it survived. Those created dramatic shifts and changes in social, economic, or political reality. The turmoil of death and destruction is exacerbated by economic disruptions, political upheaval, or social strife all of which leads to emotional overload. The societal body begins to shut down in order to heal.

"To outside forces, it appears to be apathy, but in reality, it is the first step toward healing. The next step is invariably anarchy. Somewhere after that become the first legitimate steps toward freedom. But what you are talking about suggests there is about to be another player in the game that is going to upend the status quo."

Chapter Seventy-Nine

Lane Alexander said, "Mr. Rubenstein, I have something to tell you. Mayor White has not been totally honest with you or Chief Sanderson. We found a whole lot more weapons than you have seen. We have rockets, shoulder-fired rockets of several types and all of the ammunition they require. Most fire projectiles but we have one that fires incendiary ammunition."

"Have you seen them?" Chief Sanderson asked.

"Yes, and I've seen them work. There are pretty devastating in my opinion."

"Hold on a minute. Wes, can you have that weapons specialist of yours join us? Have you got information available on shoulder-fired weapons from the 1980 Army inventory?"

"Sure we have that information. I'll get him here right away."

*****

After debriefing Alexander and pouring through pre-Night of the War archives, Sanderson picked up the phone. "Paul, meet me in the Communications Center, we need to talk… now."

It was obvious that Sanderson was troubled. "Well, my weapons guy has listened to Mr. Alexander's description and here is what he thinks they are. Number one is the M202 Flash, a 66mm, 4-tubed multi-shot incendiary rocket launcher. It weighed about twenty-six pounds loaded and could deliver a round up to 820 yards. It was designed to replace the World War II–vintage flamethrowers, such as the M1 and M2, which remained the military's standard incendiary devices well into the 1960s. The M202 was based on the prototype XM191 Napalm rocket launcher that saw extensive testing in the Vietnam War. The M202 was designed to share its 66mm caliber with the contemporary M72 LAW anti-tank rocket launcher, to allow it to be used as an anti-tank launcher.

"It is logical to assume there is a bunch of the M72 LAW or Light Anti-Tank Weapons, a portable one-shot 66-mm unguided anti-tank weapon. The M72 LAW was adopted by the Army and the Marines as their primary individual infantry anti-tank weapon, replacing the M31 rifle grenade and the M202A1 or Super Bazooka; it was subsequently adopted by the Air Force to serve in an anti-emplacement/anti-armor role in Air Base Defense duties.

"There are probably some of the M202A1s, as with most Rocket Propelled Grenades, no dedicated gunners were trained; the weapon instead being carried in addition to the rifleman's standard weapon. While vastly more lightweight than the M2 flamethrower it replaced, the weapon was still bulky to use and the ammunition suffered from reliability problems.

"From Mr. Alexander's description, I think we also have the M47 Dragon. This was an American shoulder-fired, man-portable, anti-tank missile system. The Dragon used a wire-guidance system in concert with a high explosive anti-tank warhead and was capable of defeating armored vehicles, fortified bunkers, main battle tanks, and other hardened targets. It was primarily created to defeat the Russian T-55, T-62, and T-72 tanks.

"But, this next one scares me. It is a really bad boy; the AT4 was a disposable, low-cost alternative to a recoilless rifle. It operated on the principle of a recoilless weapon, in that forward inertia of the projectile is balanced by the inertia of propellant gases ejecting from the rear of the barrel. But unlike the recoilless rifle, which used a heavier and more expensive steel tube with rifling, the disposable AT4 design greatly reduces manufacturing costs by using a reinforced smoothbore, fiberglass outer tube.

"The only real disadvantage of the recoilless design is that it creates a large back blast area behind the weapon, which can cause severe burns and overpressure injuries to friendly personnel in the vicinity of the user and sometimes even to the users themselves, especially in confined spaces and the back blast may also reveal the user's position to the enemy. It used a wide variety of ammunition and projectiles.

"There was a HEAT projectile that can penetrate up to 16.5 inches of RHA with beyond-armor effect."

"What is RHA?"

"Sorry, RHA stands for Rolled Homogeneous Armor. It is a type of armor made of a single steel composition hot-rolled to improve its material characteristics, as opposed to layered or cemented armor. Its first common application was in tanks. After World War II, it began to fall out of use on main battle tanks and other armored fighting vehicles, intended to see front-line combat as new anti-tank weapon technologies were developed which were capable of relatively easily penetrating rolled homogeneous armor plating even of significant thickness.

"Next was the HEDP 502, High Explosive Dual Purpose, the round was used against bunkers, buildings, and enemy personnel in the open and light armor. The projectile could be set to detonate on impact or with a slightly delayed detonation. The heavier nose cap allowed for the HEDP projectile to either penetrate light walls or windows and then explode, or be "skipped" off the ground for an airburst. For use against light armor, there is a smaller cone HEAT warhead with 5.9 inches of penetration against RHA.

"There was an HP or High Penetration round for extra high penetration ability of up to 19.7 inches to 23.6 inches of RHA. There was an AST or Anti Structure Tandem-warheads designed for urban warfare where a projectile heavier than the HEDP AT4 was needed. This projectile combines a HEAT warhead with a shallow cone, which results in low penetration but produces a wide hole, with a follow-through high-blast warhead. It has two settings: one for destroying bunkers and one for mouse holing a building wall for combat entry.

"There was an anti-armor version with HEAT warhead that extends range from 300 to 600 meters and a HE or High Explosive anti-personnel round that could be set for impact or airburst detonation, with an effective range of up to 1,000 meters. Paul, we are no longer talking some rednecks riding horses with hunting rifles. The first three of these weapons can take out everything we have except The Eggs and Retreat 2. That includes the AATVs, ATPAAVs, and VTOLs. It's the AT4 and the Dragon I'm worried about. I really don't think any of them can hurt an Egg when it is fully operational, but if an Egg is hit before its cloak and force field is activated... I just don't know."

"And Retreat 2?"

"Either the AT4 or the Dragon, if used correctly, could collapse the ceiling and kill everyone inside."

Chapter Eighty

"I don't know, Mr. Mayor. I think so but I can't be sure without a test."

"Now, Jacob Allen... you are one of our smartest. You have read the manual haven't you?"

"Yes, Sir."

"All of the equipment seems to be functional doesn't it?"

"Yes, Sir... once we got the batteries back up to charge."

"Then what is the problem?"

"I don't know that there is one, Mr. Mayor. Might just be the slickest thing you ever saw when we push the button and it might not work at all. The question is this... is what we have what the designers wanted? Are the power settings still good? We think they are. Is the propellant still good? We think it is. But we are not going to know until we try to fire one of these things and you said not to do it outside because they would know."

Mayor White thought for a moment. "Then we won't do it outside..."

"Mr. Mayor, we can't shoot that thing off in the Underground, there's no telling what it would do."

"Now, now, Jacob Allen..." Mayor White put his hand on the young man's shoulder. "I wouldn't shoot that in our cave. But I have another cave in mind; it used to be called Sequiota Cave and the only things that live there is a colony of gray bats. Come to think of it they might be gone now. I haven't been there in years. Long time ago it was part of a state fish hatchery. Gonna need a boat though since there's water in the cave.

"Get some of the canoes ready. I want you to take several teams to watch, show them how to do it, you know? They need to know how to use these things when the time comes."

"Yes, Sir." Jacob Allen ran off to set things in motion. Mayor White watched him go and thought, *Yes, Siree Bob, they need to know how to use these things when the time comes and the time is right around the corner. I can just about guarantee that.*

Chapter Eighty-One

As Roderick van Arnstein shook Colonel Mikhail Sergeyevich's hand, he passed a note to the Russian. Moments later, Sergeyevich read, "Meet me in the garden after this." When Roderick van Arnstein looked at him again Sergeyevich nodded *surreptitiously.*

*****

Mikhail had hoped that van Arnstein was simply relaying a message to him from his sister... instead, Roderick himself walked quickly out of the main house and walked toward Sergeyevich. "Thank you for meeting me, Colonel."

Clicking his heels and bowing slightly, Sergeyevich asked, "How may I be of service to you, Sir?"

Sergeyevich was not a small man himself and was not without strength and speed, but Roderick van Arnstein moved faster than the eye could see, grabbing Mikhail by the throat and lifting. Roderick's fingers clinched unerringly around Sergeyevich's Adam's apple; he squeezed and lifted. Mikhail found himself standing on his tiptoes barely able to breathe.

Roderick leaned in close and whispered, "First, you will stay away from my sister AND you will ensure that she stays away from you. I shall hold you personally responsible should either of you make contact with the other. Do I make myself understood?"

Mikhail tried to speak but could not, tried to nod but could not and finally settled for mouthing "Yes." Roderick loosened his grip by degrees and Mikhail was able to breathe again.

"Second, it is time for this charade to end. Bring me your Commanding Officer. I wish to ensure that he and your Russian command understand who is actually in charge, both right at this moment and when the world is under one control."

Chapter Eighty-Two

Wes Sanderson's comm unit beeped; the message read, "Report to the Communication Center… 911." He turned and began to double time across the field and back toward Retreat 2.

Entering the cavern, he headed toward the Communication Center and jerked open the door. "What's up, Master Sergeant?"

Master Sergeant Lancon pointed toward the two monitor screens. "Better have a look at this Chief. We either have unannounced visitors or trouble and based on their movements, I suggest trouble."

Sanderson moved in front of the two monitors. "How far out?"

"Thirty-five to forty-five minutes, give or take a few."

On the screen, Sanderson could see five groups of horsemen approaching supported by five buckboards. "Master Sergeant, can you get any closer to one of those buckboards. Can we see what they are carrying?"

"Sure thing, Chief." Lancon focused on one wagon and increased magnification.

"People and military-style cases…Chief, those look like rocket cases to me," Lancon ventured.

"Switch to a close up on one of the riders."

At random, Master Sergeant Lancon pulled in on a rider. "Holy crap, are those what I think they are?"

"Check the others, Lancon."

Scanning between the several groups of riders confirmed what Sanderson feared. "Get Paul Rubenstein and Ryan Fleming in here right now. Put the area on alert and have the motor pool rev up the AATVs and ATPAAVs. Alert the Dog Soldiers and the POTUS Posse to draw weapons."

*****

Rubenstein and Fleming entered the Comm Center from opposite ends of the center. "What is it?" Rubenstein asked. Sanderson waved them over and pointed at the monitors.

"Bloody hell!" Fleming exclaimed. "What do the buggers think they're doing?"

"I don't know but what it looks like they ARE doing is getting ready to attack us," Sanderson said. "There are five groups of ten riders each and it appears that each rider is packing either an M-16 or an M-14 with two bandoleers of ammo... plus each horse is rigged with modified saddlebags that are carrying four of what appear to be LAWs rockets."

"And what the bloody hell is a LAW rocket?" Fleming demanded.

Sanderson explained, "M72 LAW or Light Anti-Tank Weapon, a portable one-shot 66 mm unguided anti-tank weapon. Before the Night of the War, it was the primary individual infantry anti-tank weapon for both the Army and Marine Corps. The rocket detonates on impact and the effective range is 200 meters."

"The five buckboards appear to have additional rockets for resupply to the riders," Fleming added.

"The extra cases appear to be of several different sizes..." Paul commented.

"I suspect they have brought several different types of munitions," Sanderson said.

"By munitions, you mean rockets?"

Sanderson nodded. "Yep. Paul, I want you to gather up the Dog Soldiers and get them on AATVs and intercept the approaching force here." He indicated a spot on the map. "Ryan, I want you to get the Posse mounted on the ATPAAVs. They are more robust and can carry more. I want the Dog Soldiers to intercept and engage... I want you to load up and act as the hammer to smash them on the anvil the Dog Soldiers create. I'm going to maintain my Marines here as security for Retreat 2."

Chapter Eighty-Three

Paul, along with the Dog Soldiers, had set a trap for the advancing riders. Dog Soldiers... Paul smiled and remembered how they had been created and why. Thirty-four clones, cloned from the original crew members of the Eden Project, had been captured and imprisoned. The man that would be their leader, Akiro Kuriname, was a clone also. But Akiro had been taken prisoner by John Rourke.

Rourke long suspected that the clones were controlled by some unknown mechanism within the strange tattoo each wore on the left side of their chest. Rourke had removed Akiro's when he had captured him and when the decision was made to at least attempt to salvage those thirty-four souls imprisoned at the Ambrose Federal Detention Center. Oneirogenic, a general anesthetic, the formal name for sleeping gas had been pumped into the cell blocks and rendered them unconscious. The removal of all of the alien tattoos took less than three hours; once removed each tissue sample had been placed in stasis for later study and analysis.

Next to Paul's AATV was Benjamin Nehen, the Dog Soldier that was over the left wing of the ambush, dark skinned with high cheekbones and jet black hair but in a short buzz. Darrell Avonaco, whose men were responsible for the ambush's right wing was shorter and stockier than Ben. Their DNA went all of the way back to the Plains Indians, specifically the Cheyenne. Darrell's name, Avonaco, meant Leaning Bear, and at the moment he was leaning on Paul's vehicle. "They should be here in another twenty minutes or so, my scout reports they stopped for a rest break; probably have been riding since before dawn."

Paul nodded. "Okay, you two get back to your men. Darrell, remember to wait on them to be in the pocket before you spring the attack. We want to drive them toward Ben, then Ben's people will open up and that should drive them toward the only escape route left. I'll be waiting there with my force." Darrell said something in his native tongue to Ben and jogged off to take his place.

Paul smiled. "What did he say? Was that Cheyenne for good luck or something?"

Ben smiled. "No, Paul, it was Cheyenne for 'I am an Indian being told by a white man how to ambush other white men.' What a world we live in."

*****

As the AATVs were leaving to engage the approaching forces, the ATPAAVs were still being modified. Three were being changed to the Griffin configuration. They would fly in above the battleground in a surprise attack. Each Griffin had not only limited flight capabilities but was, in fact, an all-terrain dune buggy that could take off and land powered or paraglide and soar without its engine being on. Against a modern, well-equipped army, even the Griffin had limits, but against a cavalry unit with buckboards... it could be a game changer.

Fleming was a pilot as were Patrick Haryett and Earl Burger. Each was attaching a parasail to hook up points at the top of their respective Griffin and then stretched the parasail out behind the craft. Haryett reminded the other two, "Don't forget... you have a ceiling of a little over 10,000 feet and about three hours of powered flight time. Ryan, are you sure you just want the machine guns... no rockets on this mission?

"Yeah, if we hit the blokes hard after the Dog Soldiers have them engaged... it should be a wham, bam... thank ya very much, Ma'am. Game over and we meet back at the pub."

"Ryan, we don't have a pub," Earl reminded him.

Ryan winked. "True, but we do have a couple of pints, me Bucko. I'll take Spivey with me as a gunner. Patrick, you take Vaughn, as a hunting guide, he has experience firing at ground targets from altitude."

"I'm taking David Lynn to be my gunner and I can at least have an intelligent conversation with him before and after the battle... unlike the gibberish I get from you two," Earl Burger said.

Sanderson came up toting three canvas shoulder bags; he gave one to each of the pilots. "Grenades, probably more psychological than tactical but they should spice things up on the ground. If you drop them, drop from 300 feet or so then gun the engine and get well beyond the blast range. These have an advertised effective kill zone radius of five meters, with the casualty-inducing radius of about fifteen meters. Within this range, people are generally injured badly enough to effectively render them harmless. I am more concerned with shrapnel tearing through the fabric on you parasail and dropping you to the ground."

Fleming slung one bag over his neck and climbed in the ATPAAV. "Alright, Gentlemen... let's give them hell." He keyed the ignition and with the help of two members of the ground crew filled the parasail and released the brake. Moments later, a dark arrowhead formation moved across the sky to collide with the attackers. In the distance, above the muffled motor of his Griffin, Fleming could already hear the sounds of battle.

Chapter Eighty-Four

Paul watched the drone feed on the screen of his AATV. The approaching forces had changed their formation. Instead of five separate columns of riders, each with a wagon assigned, the three center columns had coalesced into one large one, and the two outside columns had dropped to the position of a quick reaction force that they could maneuver in either direction as needed. The wagons had moved to a reserve position several hundred yards back.

The center column entered the trap, not a shot was fired by the Dog Soldiers. Paul smiled. *This is gonna work.* The center column continued without incident for several minutes... then all hell broke loose from Darrell Avonaco's men.

The startled horses and men were caught flat-footed and surprised. Horses and men were cut down... instructions were being shouted... horses and men were screaming as bullets tore through their bodies. The mass of confusion divided, survivors galloped off to the left as the dead and wounded lay scattered on the field. Paul estimated that ten percent of the attackers had just paid the price for aggression.

But the tab was not closed yet; after a mad gallop away from the carnage, a fusillade of slugs rose up to slam into the riders. Over the AATV screen, Paul watched as the quick reaction force... failed to quickly react. These weren't seasoned cavalry, nor were they soldiers... They were civilians, shop keepers, and workers that had been thrown to the wolves by their own people.

By this time, Paul and his force had moved into the final position. They were about to close the box on the attackers. It was a slaughter. Paul fired out the assault rifle and reloaded.

Chapter Eighty-Five

Horses were screaming, bullets were flying and men were dying. The three sides of the trap continued to inexorably close as the riders and their horses died. Suddenly, there was a sound and a flash that ripped the air.

Paul wheeled and shouted, "The damn wagons!" He signaled for three other AATVs to follow him. Switching to the communications network, he ordered them to wheel left and drive the attack while he came straight up the middle at them. Switching to the forward firing machine gun, he toggled the steering wheel mounted switch to fire it.

The smoke streamers from two rocket motors crisscrossed over Paul's vehicle and then there was only rifle fire being sporadically directed at him. Had this been a professional force of soldiers he would have been nailed, but they weren't and he had counted on that. It is one thing to shoot at targets, but he had learned long ago it was an entirely different matter when the targets are firing back.

There was a flash and the front of his AATV sailed skyward. "Rocket," he shouted to himself and hung on. When the AATV stopped rolling, Paul was upside down and hanging by his seat belt and spitting dirt. His vision cleared and he saw someone walking calmly toward him firing a rifle. *What the...* Paul thought and reached for his assault rifle. *Gone, must have lost it in the roll over.*

He reached for the Schmeisser; the shooter was getting closer. *Damn, where is it?* The man's shots were getting closer; one pinging off the frame of his vehicle. The frame mounted machine gun had been torn loose and was crumpled. The man kept walking closer and shooting.

Then he stopped and stood there and carefully aimed. He was only thirty or so yards away. *There is no way he's going to miss at this range.*

Paul realized the left side of his chest hurt... *the Browning!* He unsnapped the strap and jerked the weapon, thumb cocking it on the way out. He fired... a miss. He fired again... a miss. *Breathing, sight picture, trigger control*, his mind shouted as he pushed the wire frame glasses back into position on his nose. *Might help if I could see!*

The Browning bucked. Paul looked into the shooter's eyes and saw a flinch. Paul closed his eyes expecting to be slammed back against his seat by the slug. The man's rifle fired.

Paul opened his eyes. The shooter was sitting on both knees. The rifle was lying on the ground; blood was oozing out of a wound in the man's chest. Paul pulled his knife from his harness and cut the seatbelt then crawled out of the wreck. He stood weakly and with the barrel of the Browning pointed at the man that walked toward him. "Don't move... don't move or I'll kill you," Paul warned.

The shooter nodded weakly. "I won't. I'm sorry."

As Paul drew closer, the shooter wilted like a flower, almost oozing to one side. Paul kicked the rifle away and knelt by the man and patted him down for another weapon. The man smiled. "I thought I could do it."

"Do what?"

"Mayor White told us we had to protect our people and that at the moment of truth we would be able to do what was necessary. It almost worked. As long as I was firing at your machine, I was fine... I could do it. But, when you looked at me and I saw your eyes... I realized... this is not a machine; it is a man... a man like me, a man that has not done anything to me except shoot me because I was shooting at him. I'm sorry..."

The man took a deep breath and slowly let it out and when it left it took his life force with it.

Paul turned, another man was running at him. No gun this time, just a large brush knife with almost twenty-inches of a curved, forged, and double-edged, razor-sharp blade and a three-foot wooden handle. He had seen this kind of blade used to harvest sugar cane and clear land. Swung correctly it could take his head off with one swing.

Up came the Hi-Power. "Hurry!" Paul's fear shouting but his training whispered, *breathing, sight picture, trigger control.* Blam, blam... the Hi-Power coughed and two 115 grain slugs hit the man. The first hit him at the junction of his neck and left shoulder tipping him back and started a spin to the left. The brush knife flew from his hands. The second slug caught him in the throat just to the right of his Adam's apple. It blew out his neck creating a pink fountain but the man was already dead.

Everything was still. Paul looked around; at first, he thought he had lost his hearing... but there was nothing to hear. The First Battle of Sac River was over. Of the fifty-five men that had attempted to attack Retreat 2, eight lay dead where the first part of the ambush was sprung. Thirty-three would be buried where they fell when the second part of the trap was sprung. Twelve more had perished when the third part of the trap sprung and in the fight with the wagon masters. Paul himself had apparently killed the last two of the attackers.

Six Dog Soldiers were injured; four from shrapnel from exploding rockets and two were injured when one of the AATVs collided with another during the heat of battle. Two injuries appeared serious but not life-threatening. Ben Nehen and Darrell Avonaco walked up to Paul's wrecked vehicle. With Ben grabbing the frame and Darrell and Paul pushing from the other side, they were able to right the AATV.

When Paul tried the key, the motor started. Darrell Avonaco spoke again in Cherokee and patted Paul's shoulder before walking off to gather his men. "What did he say this time? White man almost got scalped?"

Ben smiled. "No, actually he complimented you. He said, 'White man might make good Indian someday.'"

Chapter Eighty-Six

Captain Grigori Vadimovich Ragulin stood where he had often stood and watched her. They had almost grown up together, separated only by the cultures they had been born into and the distances between their social standings. She was Lady Wu, mystical and magical. He was a soldier without an army and a sailor without a sea.

Both trapped, prisoners of what they were but mostly of what they would never be; free.

There were times when he stood here that he thought she knew he was there. In his mind, he could convince himself that she enjoyed knowing he stood and watched for her.

Sometimes, he would be standing there in the garden looking up at her room when she would appear on the balcony.

At first, he had stepped back behind the latticework to keep her from seeing him. Eventually, he stopped stepping back and stood there for her to look at. But, she never did... never did look at him. But he was convinced that she knew he was there.

He had been with other women, Russian women... children of the children of children from the original detachment that had come here so long ago before the Night of the War. He and Lady Wu had discussed the people of the City and why and how they had remained healthy and normal throughout the centuries. Under normal circumstances, the continual gene pool could not have survived the necessities of enforced inbreeding within a closed genetic pool such as this.

But it had not been normal circumstances that had necessitated the creation of this, the third and last of the fabled Chinese Cities. Grigori often speculated how it had all come to pass. How had the two bastions of communism colluded to make such a city exist? What had happened to allow Chinese Taoist to gain control and how had the Russian delegation lost the fundamental aspects of their mission.

Long ago, when Karamatsov lived, it appeared the two factions would return to whatever the fundamental aspects of their mission had been. World domination was one. Destruction of the enemies was another. If it had not been for the "treatments," all of the inhabitants of this city would have been reduced to a barbaric madness and physical depravation that would have rendered them only slightly more than animals... if they could have even survived.

But because of those treatments, there was beauty, art, music and... life. As painful as the treatments were, the results were worth the pain.

What were the chances that between two militant governments there would be two leaders that had, independently from each other... discovered a truth, The Tao? One leader had spent his entire life in the study of the ancient traditions of philosophy and religious belief that are deeply rooted in Chinese customs and worldview. The other was a warrior who had studied Tai Chi Chuan, Qigong, and various martial arts.

When the end of the world had come, when the atmosphere had burned... two cultures had been sealed together and by virtue of that sealing, both destroyed each other and yet, gave each other a lifeline to form a better world.

Chapter Eighty-Seven

After the next fencing class, John Rourke and Grigori went back to the steam room. "Fencing has been in my family since before my ancestor the Admiral came to this Underground City so long ago. He was once a member of the largest Russian fencing school and competed in many matches. All of the equipment we have here is from him."

Rourke sat up straight and inhaled the warm steam; the towel around his waist protected his buttocks and his back still sore from when he had accidentally leaned back on the stone wall. "I think I could actually become good at fencing."

Grigori laughed. "You can become better my friend but you are too old to really become good. Your training should have started decades ago… or in your case, centuries ago." They both laughed. "You know of my ancestors, tell me about yours."

Rourke shrugged. "Not much to tell I am afraid. My family did not have the pedigree yours does. My father, his name was Thomas Lee Rourke. The name Lee came from his father… a man I never met. Dad was everything I am not and I became everything he said he wanted to be.

"His father Lee had fought in World War I in France; he was gassed in the trenches and never truly recovered. The constant artillery barrages had all but destroyed his hearing and my father told me that his father was terribly scarred by the gas and had lost his teeth. The mustard gas had pretty well destroyed his lungs and he suffered greatly and constantly. About the only sense he really had left was sight. He could see and therefore, he could read.

"My grandmother, Katherine, took over after Grandpaw Lee returned from the war; she was twenty-three at the time. She went to work and

Grandpaw stayed home to take care of my father, Thomas. They were extremely close because Grandpaw Lee had to function as both father and mother. Grandmaw Katherine lost a lot of time with my dad. They really were not close until after Grandpaw Lee passed away.

"Grandpaw Lee was adamant that my father should not serve in the military, even the National Guard. Grandpaw Lee had been in the Guard when he was called up to serve in the Great War... The war to end all wars... what a noble calling.

"But the war was not great; it was brutal, mind numbing and soul killing. And it did not end all wars... what it ended was hope and the future for an entire generation of young American boys that thought it all a great adventure to go save the world. Throughout the remainder of his life, Grandpaw Lee wondered if the world really deserved being saved.

"Had he still been alive when World War II started, he would have known it did not deserve being saved.

"My father was indoctrinated by his father. He was indoctrinated never to serve in the military and to find a way to medically help his father. While he was never trained in the medical sciences, before Grandpaw Lee passed away, my father, Thomas, could change and dress bandages, and debride dead tissue from his arms and legs. There is no telling how many times my father prevented his father from developing gangrene.

"My father had gone to classes to learn and had performed the newly developed artificial respiration on his father several times. Studying essential oils and compounds, he even developed a soothing aromatic humidifier recipe that helped his father breathe.

"Once an active and energetic man who had been over six feet tall and 225 pounds of lean muscle when he was drafted, my Grandpaw Lee died at forty years of age, weighing 115 pounds and stooped so badly he walked almost doubled over... when he was able to walk which was not often. But Lee and Thomas read and studied and went on great adventures, although they never left the upstairs flat that Grandmaw worked so hard to keep her family in.

"Her parents had died during the 1889–1890 flu pandemic that killed about a million people worldwide. Even science could not figure out what to call it, with some identifying the pandemic as the Asiatic flu and others calling it the Russian flu.

"Grandmaw Kate, as we called her, outlived her husband by thirty-five years. In all the time I knew her I never saw her laugh, but I never heard her complain. I think she was just exhausted. I think her soul gave out before her body did.

"My father and I had four conversations about those early years before Grandmaw Kate came to live with us. I remember each one and I learned something vital during each; different but vital things that had shaped my father's life and therefore shaped mine. While my Grandpaw Lee had taught my father about adventure and learning, Grandmaw Kate taught him a work ethic and inner strength he passed on to me.

"The two of them taught him about love, the love between a man and woman who kept the faith and faced the world together. Neither doing what they thought they would do with their lives but each doing what they could with their lives. In many ways, as hard as their lives were… they were lucky. Luckier than me, they found something I have only glimpsed, touched for a few moments or a few years and then watched it drift away."

"What was that, John?" Grigori asked not sure what else to say.

John Thomas Rourke looked at him with incredulity and said simply, "Why, love."

"Your mother… tell me about her?"

John smiled. "As my dad would tell me a hundred times… 'She was special.' Her name was Marie and she laughed, boy could she laugh.

She and Grandmaw Kate were close. I think because Mom was an orphan, too. Her parents and most of her family were killed when a hurricane hit Lake Okeechobee, Florida in 1928. The unnamed storm first struck Puerto Rico and killed 1,000 people. Then with 125 miles per hour winds, it hit Florida.

"Forty miles inland from the coast, rain-filled Lake Okeechobee to the brim and the dikes crumbled. Water rushed onto the swampy farmland, and homes and people were swept away. Almost 2,000 people perished.

"Her mother had not wanted to leave the house. If there's going to be a storm, she remembers her mother saying, they would be safer in the house than running away in a car. And so they gathered the family and aunts, uncles, cousins, nineteen in all, and settled down to ride out the storm.

"That night at about 8:30, the hurricane's eye passed over the lake's southeast corner. Thirty minutes later a small little five-foot dike around the lake gave way and sent six feet of water pouring into the town. It had been built to protect crops from summer rains, not a full-blown chaos flood.

"At Mom's house, someone cut an escape hatch in the roof with an ax kept in the attic for that very purpose. The piano was moved under the hole and up they climbed to escape the rising water. The house was knocked off its foundation and floated off on the raging flood, while Mom hung on for her life.

"She held on to the roof and called out to her mother, and her mother would answer. Finally, after a while, she didn't answer anymore. Mom survived as did a couple of cousins… everyone else died. It only took an hour after the dike gave way for floodwaters to peak at a fatal twelve feet. Their bodies and a lot of others were never found.

"Strange but if it had not been for the hurricane and the death of her family, she would have never met my father. She went to live with an uncle in Illinois and later met this young man who was named Thomas Lee Rourke or I would have never been born."

Grigori said, smiling, "And if you had not been born, none of your family and a lot of the population of the world would not be here today. It is amazing how fate and luck and destiny are all tied together some times. Events from halfway around the world or halfway across the country somehow get tied together and a story begins that becomes not just a life but a whole series of lives."

Chapter Eighty-Eight

General Thorne met with the KI Commander. "Commander, if we are going to be allies, I'd like to have an appreciation of the capabilities of your craft and an understanding of their weaponry."

"General, I think that is reasonable. If we are going to fly and fight together, we should understand what each other is capable of. Would you like to take a ride in my craft first?"

"Yes, Commander I would."

*****

General Thorne called Akiro Kuriname to the Operations Center. "Akiro, I'm going to take a ride with the KI Commander in his ship."

Akiro frowned. "By yourself? Do you think that is a good idea?"

Thorne smiled. "I don't know and there is only one way to find that out. But that is why I'm telling you about it. I want you in your ship and launched before Crenshaw and I take off. I want you to monitor our flight and if things start to look like they are going south, I want you to lock a tractor beam on that KI craft and bring us all right back here. Furthermore, until further notice I want to double the guards on the KI that came in with Crenshaw."

"You really don't trust them?"

"I don't know whether or not we can trust them, Akiro. Trust should not be given, it should be earned and right now... they haven't earned it."

"Are you going armed?"

General Rodney Thorne laughed. "Akiro, I go everywhere armed; even the bathroom."

Chapter Eighty-Nine

The KI vehicles were substantially larger than The Eggs. Each carried a four-man crew: the pilot and co-pilot, a Communications Officer and a Weapons Officer. If things got hairy, Thorne was already outnumbered four to one and each of the KI was as large as the Commander. Rodney Thorne barely came to the top of the Commander's shoulder. As the KI crew and Thorne walked toward the KI craft, Thorne snickered at the picture they made.

The KI crewmembers were efficient and professional. As the Commander did his walk around the craft, they were already checking internal systems and circuits. Thorne stayed with the Commander as they walked around the outside of the craft and the Commander explained the parts and functions of the craft.

"What is the fuel source?" Thorne asked.

"The simplest description you would understand is… Never mind, just call it a plasma drive; all of our ships, large or small have the same propulsion drive. It was developed long before we left Earth. In fact, we continue today to use the same plasma that we had then."

"You are saying there is no need to refuel?"

The Commander smiled. "None, our fuel self generates as a part of the propulsion process."

"Amazing," Thorne said. "Is that the same system that powers your weapons?"

Crenshaw nodded. "Yes, the plasma that propels the ship also powers the weapons but during the circulation process, a part of the plasma is enhanced in a special chamber of each weapon system. It is as though the ship is the weapon and the weapon is the ship; the two are linked inexorably together. That power system also powers our sensors, communications… everything."

Thorne shook his head. "And it never runs out…"

Crenshaw smiled, something the KI rarely did but he was copying from the humans; Crenshaw had a sense of humor. "It has not yet. Shall we go?"

*****

The preflight completed, Rodney Thorne took the co-pilot's seat next to the Commander. The co-pilot flipped a switch and a secondary seat folded out of the main console near the Communications Officer's station.

The Communications Officer asked the Commander, "Sir, for the purposes of take-off and operations… who do I communicate with now? I assume it is not the KI Control Center?"

"Correct, communicate with General Thorne's people instead. We are now working with them. Do not initiate any communications to the KI and do not under any circumstances reply to any they initiate. Communications Officer, request permission to take off. Weapons Officer, bring all weapons online and on standby. Co-pilot, once we have permission to launch, take the ship out of the tunnel and into open sky. Weapons Officer, engage the cloaking device as we clear the tunnel."

Thorne noticed there were no responses from the crew members to their instructions, they simply complied. In short order, the large ship had moved quietly and quickly down the tunnel finally emerging in the Arctic wilderness near to the old Mount Denali National Park. Thorne was surprised to find the KI ship had no more vibration or motor noise than his Egg did. Additionally, he had never suspected that the control systems on the two craft would be so similar; holographic imaging and mental linkages to the crew, too much similarity in technology to be either an accident or a coincidence.

The Creator's race had been involved in the development of this craft and since the Commander had said all of the KI craft were similar... it would be logical to postulate the Creator's people had also had a hand in the development of the KI Armada. Interesting for two cultures supposedly at war with each other, Thorne decided.

The Commander spoke, putting an end to Thorne's private ponderings. "Where would you like to go, General?"

"Are your cloaking devices active?" Thorne asked as he checked his wristwatch.

"Yes, Sir... they are."

Thorne nodded. "Communications Officer, please contact my base and confirm status."

The Commander turned. "I am not familiar with that terminology, General. What does confirm status mean?"

Thorne smiled. "It means, Commander, I want to make sure we can track your craft even with the cloaking device active."

"I can assure you, General, your sensors will not be able to track us when we are cloaked."

"Communications Officer, comply with my instructions and put your system on speaker. Your call sign will be Angel One for this mission," Thorne said, smiling.

The Communications Officer looked at the Commander who gave a slight nod. "Pyramid Base this is Angel One."

"Go ahead Angel One, we read you loud and clear and have you on our scope."

The Commander turned slowly toward Thorne. "How?"

Thorne simply smiled. "Now, Commander, I'd like for you to show me where you would have landed during the invasion if you had not been directed to us."

"General, if you have disabled our cloak, the Russians will see us and attack."

"No Commander, we disabled nothing. We simply enhanced our abilities to detect you, Thorne said."

The Commander nodded. "General, I hope you are being truthful. Otherwise, you should be prepared for the Russians or our other KI ships to destroy us."

"Understood, trust me, Commander. Let's go see the Russian base."

The Commander nodded to the co-pilot. "You have heard the General, comply."

Chapter Ninety

Lane Alexander and Noah had, in fact, returned to the Underground in time for one of Mayor White's reoccurring speeches. Lane told Noah where to be when the speech ended.

Alexander was shocked to see Mayor White's physical appearance; his hair was unkempt, his gait was unsteady and his skin had a ghastly pallor. He cleared his throat and began, "There are some axioms we must remember. The first is 'If you want peace, you must prepare for war.' It is rare that an intelligent nation decides to wage war, most of the time it is simply forced on you by circumstances and those circumstances always occur at the worst possible time and in the worst possible conditions.

"Therefore if you have not anticipated and if you have not prepared and have not thought about the unthinkable... you and your people will be in trouble. I have tried to do that and I think that we have arrived at the place where we must take action. We must strike the first blow rather than wait for the first blow to be struck against us.

Mayor White had written a good speech, it chronicled the First Battle of Sac River and the death of fifty-five men from the Underground who would not be back or ever hold their children or spouses again. He thought it sounded pretty good in fact... of course, it would have sounded better had they inflicted any damage on those of Retreat 2.

Lane listened and shook his head. It was obvious that White was at best delusional and at worst, self-destructive. But the problem with those that are self-destructive is they destroy others as they destroy themselves.

"Fighting a defensive war, one where you were struck rather that you did the striking... well, that may give you the positive image of defending your homeland and your citizens, and while those can often make the difference in a close battle... they seldom have much meaning when your people are already being slaughtered and your homes laid waste and burning.

"We initiated a buildup of offensive weapons that have been designed to be purely defensive. I fear, however, that now is the time to act; sometimes the worst road may be the best or only route to battle.

"Victory favors the bold and we must be bold. While we outnumber our enemy, they have skills we do not have."

"Excuse me, Mr. Mayor…"

"Yes, Citizen Alexander."

"How can we define Retreat 2 as our enemy? Outside of the initial contact, where one of our people died in an ill-advised attack on their people… they have been solicitous and friendly."

White smiled. "You are correct, they have been, and therefore they will not expect our attack or be prepared for it. We must consider the facts that by their own admissions, Retreat 2 is populated by warriors; people who have been trained to fight and wage war and to kill. We have not been, nor do we claim to have been. Our resources are limited and our skills… even more so."

Alexander raised his hand again. "So our lack of experience and lack of training and lack of equipment dictates we must attack those with more experience and more training? I fail to see the logic of that."

"No, it is true we have limited experience and training but we have a wealth of equipment, specifically the rockets that can make up the difference and an almost single-handed guarantee our victory."

Alexander shook his head. "Alright tell me, what does this victory look like in your mind? How many people do you expect we will lose and to what end? What will be different after this battle than before it?"

"Why it should be obvious," Mayor White said with a smile, "we will have won and they will have lost. We will still be here and they shall all be dead."

Alexander slowly made his way to the edge of the crowd, found his son, Noah, and hurried away. "Noah, I want you to get our horses and fill the saddlebags with food and ammunition and meet me by the old rail yard outside The Underground. Go, be there in an hour and wait for me."

*****

"I'm telling you men," Lane Alexander said. "We will not win against the people of Retreat 2. If we attacked at two in the morning with everything we had... maybe, but they would have to be asleep, sound asleep and our attack would have to be massive and dynamic. Otherwise... we're all going to die and for what?"

"We can't go against the Mayor," someone at the rear of the room shouted. "He'll be upset with us."

"And we best not go after the people in Retreat 2 or we'll be dead," Alexander said. "Each of you has to make up your own mind, mine is made up. My boy and I are leaving, I hope you will stay home and not participate in this madness. Noah and I will return after the Mayor leaves and pray everyone will come back without attacking."

Chapter Ninety-One

Master Sergeant Lancon keyed the microphone. "Chief, Lancon here. Can you come to the Communications Center ASAP?"

"On my way."

Wes Sanderson came jogging into the Communications Center. "What have you got, Master Sergeant Lancon?"

"Take a look, Sir." Sanderson studied the screen for a moment.

"Looks like another attack formation to me. Classic three-prong attack."

Lancon concurred. "That's what it looked like to me. You've got about forty minutes before they get here."

Sanderson keyed his microphone and gave orders for First and Second Platoons to bring all available AATVs to the staging point and prepare two of the ATPAAVs configured into the Griffin package. The Griffin package gave each ATPAAV limited flight capabilities with an operational ceiling of over 10,000 feet. They would be able to take off in just 330 feet and land in under 33 feet, even on poorly prepared fields.

One or two people could stay in the air up to three hours at speeds between 35 to 50 miles per hour. The vehicle's special mufflers gave silent propellers that ensured a stealthy approach. Should it be necessary to land to fight, each could do land speeds of about 65 miles per hour, while loaded with about 550 pounds of cargo to include weapons ranging from machine guns to light multi-role missiles. Each was powered by a 125 horsepower one-liter turbocharged three-cylinder engine.

In less than ten minutes the Griffins launched and climbed to an attack altitude while two, three-vehicle teams chewed up grass and dirt to meet the approaching mounted men.

*****

The AATVs crested the last hill and all hell broke loose. A shoulder fired M202 Flash belched out one of its 66mm incendiary rockets from a range of a little over 800 yards. Luckily, it went over the advancing AATVs and exploded harmlessly to the rear of the formation, only to be followed by a fusillade of M72 LAW—Light Anti-Tank Weapons rockets.

Four of the mounted horsemen had dismounted, aimed, and fired, and dropped the expended launchers before swinging back into the saddle and firing M16A2s at a full gallop.

Sergeant Bill Parish's AATV was rolled by an explosion that hit low in front of the right front side and flipped the vehicle. The gunner was ejected but rolled quickly to his feet and began engaging the enemy riders. Standing shakily, he drew his service pistol and spun to the right.

One of the riders had fired out his M-16A2 and dropped the weapon to hang from its sling. He reached low and jerked a long handled brush clearing hook from a scabbard on his saddle. The hook, normally a farm implement, was a powerful tool that could handle almost anything, that could include separating Bill Parish's head from his shoulder. A heavy hooked, doubled-edged blade atop the long wooden handle, this slashing hook quickly built momentum capable of chopping limbs and brush with ease.

Combined with the speed of the swing and velocity of a running horse, the blade would be unstoppable; the blade but not the man swinging it. Parish leaned against the chassis of the overturned AATV to steady himself. His left arm hung useless at his side but his right was fully extended in classic shooter's stance. He fired... and missed. He fired again… another miss. Parish took a deep breath, let some out and squeezed the trigger again and again and again.

The first shot was a miss but shots two and three smashed into the rider's throat and chest. The throat shot was to the right of the Adam's apple and tore through the carotid artery; the 9mm full metal jacket slug tearing through muscle and tissue before exploding out the back of the neck. The long handled brush clearing hook went flying from the man's hand.

The second 9mm slug entered the man's chest. It would have penetrated the lung and probably the man would have survived, except the first round had spun him slightly in the saddle upon impact. The slug entered his chest at an angle that smashed through a rib, ripping through the left lung before tearing through the juncture of the left atrium and left ventricle of his heart, and exiting his back as he fell from the saddle.

No longer controlled by the now dead rider, the terrified horse screamed and turned, and at full speed disappeared over the top of a small hillock.

Mayor White's riders were functioning as a pretty good cavalry. They apparently worked in teams of six; four with M72s on another rocket platform, and two riders that both held the dismounted horses and provided covering fire with automatic rifles.

Two other AATVs were hit; one was caught head-on by a 66mm unguided rocket. It was blasted to bits, the crew instantly killed. Machine guns from the advancing AATVs slaughtered men and horses alike. The screams of dying men and horses mixed with the scream of the 125 horsepower one-liter engines as the twin ATPAAV Griffins dove to the attack.

Sanderson had to give credit to the horse soldiers, what they lacked in tactics they made up for in guts. They didn't quit, that was for sure. In fact, Sanderson watched fascinated as a team of six horsemen set a course directly for his AATV. Keying his throat mic, "Hawk One, Bird Dog, I have a bogie on a collision course... can you take him out? Over."

"Bird Dog, not in time. Hawk Two and I are engaged on the wrong side of the hill, watch your ass. Out."

Sanderson cursed and slammed his foot down hard on the accelerator. The AATV leaped forward running full out at the advancing horsemen. "Alright Gunner, it is up to you and me. I'll line 'em up, you take 'em out and don't miss." The AATV dropped into a small depression before rocketing upward. Just as it topped the rise there was a man standing directly in its path. One of White's cavalrymen had dismounted to fire his rocket. He was looking through the viewfinder of an M79 Grenade Launcher when Sanderson's vehicle suddenly appeared in his sights.

Sanderson had no time to react, the AATV went airborne and slammed into the cavalryman chest high, crushing ribs and breaking one arm. The M79 never fired but tumbled through the air before breaking when it smashed into a large boulder. The man was slammed backward by the impact; the chest pack that carried grenades for the M79 hung on the front bumper rail of the AATV, dragging him through the air like a toy doll.

When the AATV landed it landed on the man, crushing the life out of him. His body hung to the AATV for twenty feet or more before the chest pack strap broke and he fell free of the vehicle.

Light machine guns from the other AATVs opened up, spraying .223 tumblers from side to side. It was like a chain saw smashing into men and horses. Sanderson couldn't feel sorry for the men, they were trying to kill him and his men; but the horses... they didn't have a choice in this stupid game.

Sanderson switched channels on his radio. "Communications Center, Bird Dog. What does the overhead show?"

Master Sergeant Lancon came over the net, "You still have hostiles on the left, looks like about fifteen, half of them on foot. Wait a minute... scratch that, one of the Hawks just ground them up and spit them out. Checking... checking... Chief, it looks like you are clear. I'd say now would be a good time to mop things up. What you didn't kill is slinkin' back toward the Underground on foot."

"Roger Comm, Bird Dog out." Sanderson pulled the AATV over and dismounted; the battlefield looked like something from long ago. Men were dead or dying, horses were screaming and dying and already the crows and buzzards were approaching. It wouldn't be long before the coyotes slunk out of the forest for their cut of carrion.

Sanderson cursed, "Stupid... stupid sons of bitches." He dispatched a squad to put the wounded horses out of their misery with a pistol shot to the head. Later he suspected the horses weren't the only ones given a coup de grace as there were no human prisoners taken.

Sanderson had lost one AATV and its two-man crew in an explosion. Two more AATVs were damaged but salvageable. Sergeant Bill Parish's left arm had been dislocated in the wreck. His gunner had jerked it back into place and tied a sling around Parish's neck and shoulder. Four more troopers had a variety of cuts and scrapes, none of which were life-threatening. An ammo check revealed that the vehicle machine guns were almost empty, a total of seventy-five rounds total remained.

The majority of troopers had a partial magazine of carbine ammo and maybe one full magazine; some only had pistol ammo left. Had Mayor White's cavalry not broken when they did, the results could have been a lot different. Later Sanderson would report to Rubenstein, "That's the difference between farmers and Marines. Farmers may fight but they are seldom killers... Marines kill everything they fight."

Chapter Ninety-Two

Rourke added a dipper of water to the hot rocks that heated the steam room. "Tell me more about how the Russians and the Chinese worked together to create this city."

Grigori sat for a long moment collecting his thoughts and letting the steam work before he spoke. "The Taoist Monks that created the Third Chinese City were not what you would call pure Taoist. That close to the Sino-Russian border, there was more commerce and interchange of activities and ideas. And Vladmir Karamatsov was not absolutely sure when the attack on America would happen, but he was sure how that initial attack would go.

"In the months that preceded the attack, his sources became more and more convinced that the attack should not be launched because it could and probably would result in the total devastation of civilization, not just the academic possibility but a real probability. He decided that the Third Chinese City was to be a fallback position for the KGB before the Night of the War. After it was determined that the atmosphere would explode into a firestorm…"

Rourke sat up. "Wait a minute. Are you saying that the Russians knew the atmosphere would ignite?"

"Well, in fairness… no one knew it for sure, but it was accepted within the ranks of the higher-ups that yes, the attack would probably result in the conflagration."

"My God, I always figured it was simply an accidental byproduct of the war."

Grigori nodded. "Well, I guess you could say that it was but it was not an unknown possibility but rather a probability, a strong probability that it would happen. That is why so much work was done here... to prepare for that eventuality."

"So, how is the Russian state structured today?"

"Honestly, there is no true Russian state anymore. It is a confederation of loosely aligned interests joined mostly by a common language. It is more a criminal enterprise than an actual government anymore."

"A criminal enterprise with one of the world's largest armies?" Rourke asked.

"Exactly."

"Who is in charge of this criminal enterprise?"

Grigori laughed. "The KGB... who else? They are also the ones that have allied with the KI against your people."

John Rourke turned to face Grigori. "You know about the KI?"

"Of course, yours was not the only government having close encounters with the alien culture. Before the Night of the War, both America and Russia were dealing with the Aliens. It was through our interactions with the Aliens that we learned of the KI and the ancient war between the KI and the Aliens."

Rourke grew silent and suspicious. "Did you people know the KI were returning?"

"Of course," Grigori laughed. "You see, after the Night of the War and the conflagration, little remained of the world. You and your family went into cryogenic hibernation but the rest of the world had to suffer through destruction. From just a few surviving centers like this one, people watched the planet as it was dying. Even the Aliens left this world, their chlorophyll processing centers were shut down and it would be centuries before there would be enough chlorophyll to justify their reopening."

Rourke said quietly, "But the Earth did not die."

"No," Grigori said. "No, it did not. Eventually, slowly, pitifully… humans came up from the ground. They came up from shelters and they came out of the water at your Mid-Wake facility. Against all odds and with little or no explanation, mankind survived. Like the Phoenix of old rising up, a new world was born from the ashes of the old one."

Rourke said sadly, "But little has changed, has it?"

Grigori smiled. "Oh no, John… much has changed… everything has changed. Don't you see it? Now instead of working for Communist domination of the world… a New World Order is poised to take control. Think of it, fascism has been defeated. Socialism has been defeated. Communism has been defeated. Feudalism has been defeated. Literally, all of the 'isms' man ever created… gone. And soon even the only representative democracy in history shall finally die."

Rourke took a deep breath, he had to ask but at the same time… he feared to do so. "Now Grigori, where do you stand in all of this change? What does the world you want look like? Whose side are you on?"

Captain Grigori Vadimovich Ragulin laughed out loud, a booming laugh that cut through the steam in the room and bounced from the dripping walls. "Why John, I thought you would have figured that out." Then he grew deadly serious. "I want Jiang Ying Yue and a world that will let us love together. I want to hold 'the river reflection of the moon' all the rest of my life.

"I stand with you John Rourke because you are the only man that can possibly make that happen. If you are successful, my life will have meaning… if you are not successful… at least I will have died trying. If we do not stop this New World Order… the very people that initiated the latest aggression against your country, the very people that tried to kill the world seven centuries ago, the very people that revitalized the ghost of selective breeding so some men could control all men... If we do not stop them, never will you or I or the family you have or the family I wish to have… never will we win."

Rourke looked at Grigori seriously. "Does Yue know of your feelings?"

"Of course, she does," he laughed. "How would she not?"

"Have you told her?"

Grigori grew serious. "I must speak these things to her?" Rourke nodded. Grigori said, "But…" Rourke shook his head.

"Tell her, tell her now."

Chapter Ninety-Three

In the place of Lady Wu and Mistress Wu stood Jiang Ying Yue, whose name translates to 'river reflection of the moon.' Before her stood Captain Grigori Ragulin.

"How can this be?" she asked.

"I have loved you since we both were children... I thought you knew," he said.

"But I am wu... I cannot marry."

Grigori looked down at the ground. "So you do not love me?"

She was stunned and not sure what to say, so she slapped him. "You... you... I don't know what you are. All of our lives you say you have loved me and NOW you tell me. Now, when you are leaving?"

She slapped him again.

Grigori rubbed his crimson cheek and cocked one eyebrow. "So you are mad I never told you I loved you? Hmmm, if you do not love me... you won't be excited or heartbroken. You simply wouldn't care. But you are mad, mad enough to strike me." He paused for a long moment and took her gently into his arms. She resisted but only for a moment and her resistance melted.

Yue looked up at him. "You have wasted so much time; I never knew you loved me."

He smiled. "I always knew I loved you... I just assumed you knew and I hoped you might love me back. Now I know you did and you do."

She sighed. "All the things I never knew are gone. And soon you tell me that you will be gone also."

He smiled. "But I will be back..." His lips met hers for the first time. He picked her up, she was a feather. The night was long but not nearly long enough. At sunrise, he wondered if a lifetime of her would be enough.

Chapter Ninety-Four

John Thomas Rourke stood on the plains of China alongside a horse-drawn carriage; Captain Grigori Vadimovich Ragulin and Jiang Ying Yue stood next to him holding hands. "Jiang Ying Yue, you are a very lucky woman to have a man like this love you."

She smiled a shy smile. "And he is a very lucky man to have a woman like me love him."

"Yes, he is," Rourke said, smiling. "Are you sure you will not go with us?"

"I am sure. You are men and must go and do men things. I am a wu. I must prepare the invocations, the divinations and be ready to interpret the dreams and heal the world and be ready to drive off the evil spirits. My people and I must dance and become invisible so we may speak the language of the spirits."

Rourke smiled and nodded as he pulled the battered Zippo lighter from his pocket and pulled the lighter mechanism out of the case to expose a small round metallic talisman. He stuck his thumbnail into a groove on the top of the talisman and turned it a quarter turn before replacing it. "I have activated a tracking device; our ride shall be here soon. Madam Wu, it has been an honor and a privilege to meet you and I look forward to seeing you again in the near future. Until then I shall watch over Grigori with my life."

Jiang Ying Yue turned to Ragulin and stood on her tiptoes to kiss him. The kiss was long and deep. Ragulin seemed to sway momentarily, recovered and looked at her. "Never has a kiss been like that before, Yue."

"Come back to me safely, Grigori and all of my kisses will be as that one all of your life."

Dust began to swirl and a strange egg-shaped craft materialized suddenly and settled to the ground. The skin of the strange craft shone brightly in the sun and suddenly Yue recognized the shape of a door appearing on it. The door folded downward making a stair to enter the craft. Akiro Kuriname stuck his head out, waved and jokingly asked, "Someone call for a cab?"

Rourke waved back. "Yep, we did." He turned to Jiang Ying Yue and bowed slightly; she returned the bow. "Come on Grigori, give her one more kiss and make it a good one... it is going to have to last you a while." Grigori did exactly that then spun and followed Rourke to The Egg. Before the hatch raised and sealed the ship, Grigori stuck his head out and yelled, "I love you."

Jiang Ying Yue, Mistress of Wu and Sorceress of the Wing, felt a tear run down her cheek as she blew him a kiss. Then the door sealed; the ship rose and disappeared.

Chapter Ninety-Five

Grigori watched the holographic image of Yue as she mounted the carriage and turned the horse back toward the Third Chinese City. Rourke put his hand on Grigori's shoulder. "It won't be long before you see her again, my friend."

Grigori smiled. "Of course not, John Rourke... all we have to do is defeat a new world order, the largest criminal enterprise the world has ever known, manipulate a positive peace between three cultures alien to each other, and establish a system of government that is truly... how does that saying go?"

"You mean the one about a government of the people, by the people and for the people?" Rourke asked with a smile.

"Yes, that's the one."

Chapter Ninety-Six

"How is she, David?"

Dr. David Blackman, Chief of Psychological Research at Mid-Wake stood with Rourke behind the one-way mirror that allowed observation in the therapy room.

"Physically she is fine, John. She maintains a healthy exercise program; her body weight is appropriate, blood gases normal, metabolic rates optimum. Physically, she is fine."

"But..."

"But Emily Sheppard, a widow who had lost her family in the plague caused by the Very Bad Bug, a manmade genetic aberration that had killed thousands... Emily Sheppard has no memory of ever being Emma Shaw Rourke. She has no memory of her children; and John, she has no memory of you as her husband."

Chapter Ninety-Seven

"Mayor White, have you ever heard of a man named Victor Frankl?"

"No, why… what about him?"

"Oh, it is just that you and he could have some great philosophical conversations about right and wrong. He was a Jew who survived the Holocaust during World War II.

"I have been told that never happened. It is a propaganda lie spread by the Jews."

"Oh, no… it was quite real," Rubenstein said, emphatically. "I lost family members during that war, some in the extermination camps. But that no longer matters except to God. Frankl wrote a book entitled 'Man's Search for Meaning.' It told of his struggles in the concentration camps, and how Frankl liberated himself by choosing not to let himself lose hope of survival. Many others in the camps remained 'mentally enslaved by the notion that rescue was impossible or there is no more meaning to their life.' He did not.

"He did, however, lose his scruples, writing 'The best of us did not return.' He learned he had to be unscrupulous in the camps just to survive. Those that acted selflessly… died. There weren't enough supplies and if you shared… there were even fewer. The prisoners who worked with the Nazis got extra food and better treatment. They stayed alive but knew for the rest of their lives how 'unethical' they were. Why did you send your people to attack us?"

"To prevent you from attacking us, of course," White replied.

"You should not have done that. It was not necessary; we would not have attacked you. We were prepared to work together with you and your people."

"I could not take that chance. I knew it was only a matter of time before you would come to take what was ours and with your technology… how could we have stopped you?"

"Greed, fear, distrust… such petty things," Paul said. "Such poor reasons to die but oh…so very common. Do you know what else Frankl taught those who read his book? He taught us that an abnormal reaction to an abnormal situation is normal. What does he mean by this paradox? How can you relate it to a time in your own life? It means when one is living in an abnormal condition, it is normal that he also behaves abnormally. Murder is not a normal, acceptable thing. But in these circumstances, the way you chose to live has impacted the way we have chosen to live. And now, our ability to survive has been lessened by your attempt to survive."

Paul pulled the Browning Hi-Power from his battered shoulder holster and brought the hammer back to full cock. "Do you have any last words?"

White drew himself up, straight and tall and said simply, "I am sorry. I was thinking only of my people."

"I am sorry also, Mr. White. Now I must think about both of our peoples. And that is a shame." Paul pulled the trigger. White's head snapped back pulling his body with it.

Epilogue

As Kuriname approached the sliding door, it quietly hissed upward and The Creator stepped out carrying the headband. Kuriname accepted the headband and The Creator spoke. How... is... it... you... are... with... the... humans... and... so... many... of... the... Others?

"John Rourke broke the link you had to me when he removed my tattoo, and the others lost their link when their tattoos were removed."

You... no...longer... hear... Me?"

"No, I do not."

Do... you... know... this... Russian... that... works... with... the...Others?

Akiro shook his head.

The creature looked quizzically at Kuriname. What... is... it... that... you... wish... to... ask... me?

"Is there any help you can offer Rourke that will...?" Kuriname thought for a moment about how to phrase his request. "Is there any help you can offer John Rourke that will help him repair his mate's mind?"

It... is... possible... however... I... do... not... believe... he... would... be... willing... to... pay... that... price.

"What would it cost him?"

"Everything..."

*****

Sergeyevich stretched his tight muscles, it must be over soon... this waiting was excruciating. *Soon,* he thought. *Soon I can go back to Mother Russia and somehow I will make sure I'm able to take Andrea with me. We will be able to change history, she and I, and we shall share the new world together.*

*****

John Rourke stiffened as he felt the presence of another mind touch his; it was The Keeper. *John, do you trust me?*

Rourke looked around to be sure no one was within earshot before answering with his mind, *Of course... you know I do.*

Then be careful. John, there is great danger for you and your people and I may not be able to protect you. I may not even be able to protect myself. Then Rourke heard something... no, not accurate... he felt something.

Keeper... Keeper... are you alright?

Keeper... Keeper... are you alright? But there was no answer.

*****

On the other side of the world, lights flickered in the darkened cave. Inside the cryogenic chamber, the veil of what looked like smoke parted. A chest began to rise and fall; blood began to flow again in the body. The lid to the chamber hissed as the seal was broken and it rose. A pair of tight-fitting dark leather gloves rose from inside... they shook with the effort and grabbed hold of the rim of the chamber.

A dark-clad body sat up right... dark bloodshot eyes slowly opened. Eyes that had the look of madness in them...

Author's Note

As the resurrection of the Survivalist series began, I pictured a man from the KI… a man from Atlantis called The Keeper in my mind. The more I thought about him… his unusual blending of humor and seriousness, his almost mystical thought process, a man named Allan Cole came to my mind. Allan and I met in 1995, a Canadian by birth, he had served in the U.S. Air Force as I did.

Like me, he was also a student of the author of *Illusions – The Adventures of a Reluctant Messiah*, Richard Bach. For years, we had many discussions about the physical and the metaphysical; he was a very "advanced life form." I sent some ideas to Allan about The Keeper and he guided me in The Keeper's creation.

Recently, Allan's wife Joann advised us that Allan unexpectedly had passed from what should have been a minor injury.

From time to time, you may see a blue feather come drifting into your life. When you do, take a moment to think about a Canadian that became a U.S. Airman, and then a U.S. citizen, and then my friend, and then an Atlantean master called The Keeper, and then went to the next level of everything.

Allan, I'll see you when I see you, old friend.

-Bob

On Sale Now!

The Survivalist *series*

For more information
visit: www.SpeakingVolumes.us

On Sale Now!

The Survivalist *series*

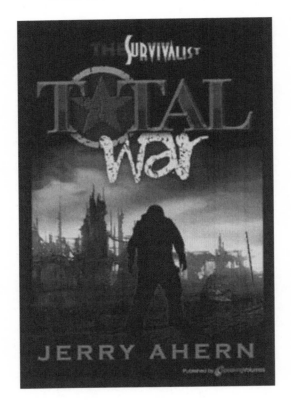

For more information
visit: www.SpeakingVolumes.us

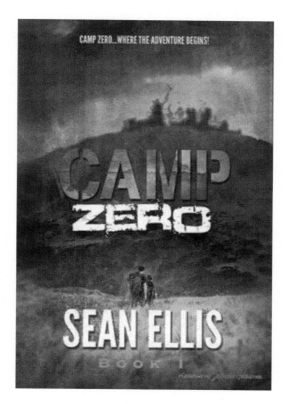

On Sale Now!

Surgical Strike *series*

For more information
visit: www.SpeakingVolumes.us

On Sale Now!

They Call Me the Mercenary *series*
Axel Kilgore (Jerry Ahern)

**For more information
visit:** <u>www.SpeakingVolumes.us</u>

On Sale Now!

The Takers *series*

**For more information
visit:** www.SpeakingVolumes.us

On Sale Now!

TAC Leader *series*

**For more information
visit:** www.SpeakingVolumes.us

50% Off
Audiobooks

As Low As $5.00 Each
While Supplies Last!

Free Shipping
(to the 48 contiguous United States)

For more information
visit: www.HalfPriceAudiobooks.com

Made in the USA
Monee, IL
01 June 2023

35114891R00166